THE LEMONADE BROTHERS

By Eddie Skelson

This book is a work of fiction. Any references to historical events, real people or real places are used fictitiously. Other names, places and events are products of the authors imagination, and any resemblance to actual events, persons or places, living or dead, or undead, is purely coincidental.

Copyright @ Eddie Skelson 2018

Cover by Mike Fyles
https://www.deviantart.com/mikefyles/

The Lemonade Brothers Copyright @ Eddie Skelson 2018

An imprint of Pandemic Press 2018
Stoke on Trent

England

Authors note

This book is the result of a piece of experimental writing I did in 2016. I challenged myself to knocking out 500-1000 words a day during the lead up to Halloween for a bit of local publicity. The end result was The Lemonade Brothers. A story featuring two men, one a middle-aged former Special Forces ultimate badass, and the other a guy who used to work in finance.

It was rough. Very rough. With no edit, no rewrite and no chance to change my mind as the story progressed I found it very challenging to keep the pace at first. Yet, as the story progressed it became much easier. The lads, Geoff and Bevvo seemed to be very confident that what they had to tell me was worth listening too. So, I did what I always do, I let them lead me around.

This new version has been edited (of a fashion) some portions removed (like the entire first chapter) and here and there some fluff that should have been dropped in the first time. Its tidied up so that the second book has a smoother transition and opens up the road to future stories. Because I know a bit of coin when I see it.

While this replaces the electronic version of The Lemonade Brothers book one you can still obtain the previous version (if you really, really want it) as a PDF directly from myself, until I get bored of emailing. Just hit me up on Facebook. Or something.

Thank you as always for coming along with me on these little trips into the dark corners of my imagination. I've plenty of others to show you.

Eddie Skelson 2017

The Lemonade Brothers
Book One

THE FUCKER

**Outskirts of Hanley Town Centre.
Stoke on Trent.**

'There.' Geoff pointed towards the multi-storey car park attached to the rear end of a cinema. The **I** and the **E** had fallen, and were nestled in the overgrown shrubs below. This left the large block capitals of **C N WORLD** displayed.

'It's a Cineworld,' Geoff thought upon seeing it.

He had been forced to watch Fifty Shades of Grey at a Cineworld with his wife when he had lost a bet. He hated Cineworld.

Lying against the edge of the small rise on the embankment facing a dual-carriageway, Geoff had spotted and mentally noted the position of every possible threat that lay immediately across that road.

At his side scanning the situation ahead of them with binoculars, Bevvo, his companion of two years, noticed the missing letters too.

'Cunt World,' Bevvo thought. His mind, as usual, working at a tangent to Geoff's.

'Third floor... see?' Geoff said.

Bevvo saw. He thought of Geoff's eyesight as thing of wonder, because he only just caught the shadows moving for a moment, and as he was using their only pair of binoculars he was impressed.

'Fuck me Geoff, you've got eyes like a shithouse rat.' he said. 'How many do you reckon?'

Geoff grimaced. He didn't like to be vague. 'At least three... but it could be dozens. That's all I saw on that level, and there could some on every floor. Probably are.'

'Yeah,' Bevvo agreed. 'Can't use it to get through then.'

'Nope.'

Geoff was disappointed in his observation, but not surprised. The Deads liked to mill around places like this, enclosed, familiar. They were drawn to town centres, and buildings like police stations, hospitals, library's, often their places of work, cafes, nightclubs, cinemas and other places of leisure. Shopping centres were Dead Central, no doubt of that. A shopping mall without a zombie was a like a Reddit subscriber without an opinion. Bevvo missed Reddit. He missed the Internet. He sorely missed PornHub.

They were here because he had been given some interesting information recently. It was the sort of intelligence that had to be taken with a pinch of salt of course, in the same way that rumours of a reformed government, air drops from European aircraft and a cure for whatever the fuck it was had caused all this horseshit being found were treated, with extreme caution. But Geoff had a good feeling about this one, at least concerning the accuracy of the intel.

The information was about a stash, a hideout located inside a small town, which had been constructed to allow its architects the ability forage the shops and businesses around the place with limited risk. It was also said that the large shopping centre that dominated the corner of the town was untouched. If the word received was true, there was some sort of method allowing safe passage through the town, perhaps a tunnel, or system of corridor's that hid people from the view of Deads. If this would give access to and from the stores it would be a very welcome find.

Apparently, this system, whatever it was, had worked well until the inevitable had occurred, someone got sloppy. People always got sloppy because they didn't stick to a plan. Geoff always stuck to the plan. Mostly.

Bevvo counted the Deads meandering up and down the dual carriageway, which lay in a dip between them, and the small bank of grass and unruly shrubs leading up to the car park. There were only five on the stretch of road that mattered, all Romeros, the slow, stupid things that staggered about, reaching to grab people who weren't there. Animated bags of dead matter with only one motivation, to eat the living.

The others, the fast ones, moved frighteningly quick and showed some degree of feral intellect. Although, they ran like absolute twats, arms flailing everywhere. These he called Danny Bees or Dannys. There were others too, it was getting to be that every foray seemed to produce a new kind of undead threat.

For the worst of them so far however, he used Geoff's preferred title, *Scooters*. Geoff had never volunteered why he called them that and Bevvo felt oddly afraid to ask. Scooters were the weirdest, scariest fucking thing he had ever encountered. The last thing he would want to bump into here was a Scooter. They moved incredibly slowly, their arms and legs twisted to strange angles, and they were as black as the night. He had never seen one close-up, he had met people who claimed they had, but he wasn't sure they were being truthful. Most stories of these things came from people who had witnessed them at a distance. A long distance.

The low number of Romeros on the carriageway wasn't surprising, they rarely walked on roads, in the same way they frequently swarmed into towns and cities. Both he and Geoff, and a number of others in the same game, had determined that it was instinct from life, guiding them in this weird state of undeath.

Looking at the set-up ahead he reckoned this band of clowns had probably tumbled down the bank and then became confused. That they were still plodding around indicated nothing had given them cause to move on.

This was good. It meant the horde was calm. And there was quite a horde. For a small place, Geoff had estimated that they could run from corner to corner of the town in less than three minutes, there were a *lot* of Deads.

'We can take these out no problem,' Bevvo said, indicating the five Romeros, 'use the trees as cover, pick em off.'

'Yeah.' Geoff replied, but sounded unsure.

'You think we'll be seen from the car park?'

'It's not that,' Geoff replied, 'it's those trees on the bank, the shrubs. If any more of these bozo's have come down they might be stuck, and are hidden by the foliage. If we go in there, and they see us coming, it might get noisy.'

'We could run back up this way though.' Bevvo replied. He thought Geoff could be over cautious, not a terrible quality to have but it did slow down the pace.

'We could.' Geoff replied, nodding as though still mulling that point, 'but the whole place will be active within seconds and any chance we had of getting in there will be gone, and I don't really fancy going back to Ashbourne empty handed.'

'You're prevaricating mate.' Bevvo said, lifting the binoculars to his eyes again. He zoomed in on the ground floor of the car park.

8

'Where the fuck did you pick up a word like that?' Geoff asked.

'I'm not just the looks in this partnership son.' Bevvo replied without taking his eyes from the binoculars.

Geoff suppressed a grin. It was typical of what he liked about Bevvo. Even in the toughest times the lad maintained a quirky, optimistic attitude. They had both been severely tested in the last three years, each facing decisions which had torn at their hearts and minds. They had come through it all though, mostly intact Geoff thought, and it was his partners irrepressible character that had been the rope to which they clung rather than his own stoic but depressed determination.

At fifty-two he was twice Bevvo's age and the distance in years seemed to work in their favour. While he was the more capable physically, Bevvo was a match for him intellectually. A smart young man with a gift for communication, not just what he said but how he said it. They would have been turned away from many an enclave and community if it hadn't been for the winning charm of Bevvo, compared to his own 'take it or leave it' attitude.

'Something's happening Gee.' Bevvo said, moving the binoculars slowly to the left and right.

'What's the rumpus?' Geoff leaned his head forwards, squinting as though it might telescope his vision.

'Dunno. They're on the move though. Your mates in the car park just started waddling off towards the entrance.'

Geoff looked down to the dual carriageway. Three of the Deads had turned their attention to the top of the bank they had probably fallen down originally.

'Yeah, something's got them agitated.'

Geoff watched as the three who had turned began to stagger towards the verge. The remaining two appeared to be oblivious and maintained their confused amble.

'You thinking what I'm thinking?' Bevvo asked, he handed the binoculars to Geoff who took them and immediately began to scan the area for further activity.

'If you're thinking that we hit these fucknuts while they are distracted and get into the car park, then yeah, we are of one mind.'

At this, Bevvo grunted his approval. He slid back from the edge of their observation spot until he was certain he couldn't be seen, as he stood and slipped off his back-pack. He walked over to the two large Bergens they had dropped, away from the embankment, and pulled out their home-made armour from each.

Between them they had fashioned arm, shin and thigh covers from tyres. They also had rudimentary neck braces. The pieces were cumbersome but offered reasonable protection against the clawing, and more importantly the biting from the Deads.

With his guards in place Bevvo strapped a pair of knives to each calf. It was impractical to wear them all the time but when there was an opportunity to prepare it was good to have the extra weapons readily available. His main method of assault was via the two ice-pick's he dropped into wide loops on his belt. They were light-weight and easy to swing with considerable force. The spiked tip could easily penetrate the skulls of the Deads. Against Romeros they were perfect, but not so much when facing even one Danny Bee. The Dannys moved quickly, and their erratic, jerking spasms threw off his aim. When going toe to toe with those he preferred his machete. It had a better reach, and if the clothing of the Dead was in tatters, if they had any at all, he was capable of removing a limb with a solid swing.

Geoff scrawled back, as Bevvo had done, and also prepared his gear. He sported a machete too, backed up by a long knife on his hip, held in a sheath made from strips of an old leather jacket. His other handcrafted item was an extremely large monkey-wrench with nine-inch nails welded to its head. He called it 'The Fucker'.

Naming their weapons was fun. Bevvo called his Ice-picks Pinky and Perky.

'That's the most gangster fucking hairbrush on the planet mate.' Bevvo said, as Geoff gave his 21st Century Morning Star a few swings to warm up his wrists and shoulders.

Bevvo often made this same quip but it always elicited a smile from Geoff.

'You want a parting in that scruffy pile of yours mate?' Geoff asked.

Bevvo almost laughed but contained it. It wasn't wise to make too much noise near the Deads. He did think he was probably overdue a haircut though.

They each secured their Bergens, wearing them tightly fastened because losing the packs would be bad. In each were survival kits, food, water and everything they needed to survive away from any ready source of nourishment or safety.

'We good?' Geoff asked.

'Yeah, let's do it.' Bevvo replied.

They strode to the edge of the embankment until they could just see over the top. The three Deads, who had made for the rise on the far side, were struggling to make it to the top. They were too stupid to use their hands to grasp the trees about them to help. On the road the other two still dithered, looking drunk and lost.

'OK, the road is yours,' Geoff said, 'I'll go for the fellas on the bank.'

'Roger that.' Bevvo replied, lifting both ice-picks from their loops. 'Don't run out of breath old man.'

'Don't mess your hair up dick head.' Geoff replied. He launched into a run down the embankment. Bevvo followed closely behind.

Geoff made directly for the Dead furthest down the bank, running straight between the two on the road. The zombies turned slowly, almost as though they couldn't believe what they had just seen fly past them. The distraction allowed Bevvo to attack them completely unseen. They were too far apart to strike both at once, but he was able to slam the pick in his right fist into the back of the head of one, and take two strides to impale the other through its temple with his left. Each creature's knees buckled immediately, indicating his blows had landed perfectly.

Geoff charged with only the one weapon in hand, keeping the other free for balance should he struggle as the Deads were with the incline. He would have preferred to use the machete here, but The Fucker was just as dangerous to him when strapped to his back, should he fall he could wind up getting spiked by his own weapon. It was best to have it where he could see it.

His first target was completely unaware of his approach and Geoff raised the wrench high and back, he then swung as though returning a shot in tennis and the wrench drove into the back of the Romero's skull shattering it completely. The Fucker drove on and out, spraying brains and bone in front of it. It truly lived up to its nickname.

Geoff used his momentum to carry on to his next target. It was dangerous here, while currently oblivious to the attack coming at them the creatures still had the high ground. Any Jedi could tell you what an advantage that offered. Rather than take the risk of attempting a single strike to the head to take them down, Geoff opted for a disabling blow.

As he approached the nearest Dead, gripping the wrench with both hands, he lifted it above his head. In one stride he was within striking distance and brought it down onto the back of the Romero's leg. The nails drove into its kneecap, the impact turning the tissue to jelly. Geoff ripped the wrench to the right and tore the whole back of the knee away, almost severing the limb.

The Dead dropped as Geoff nimbly skipped aside, and as it hit the floor the wrench was already coming around in a high arc, crashing into what remained of the zombie's already terrible face, turning its head into mush.

The final Romero began to turn. Its senses, however they worked, had finally cottoned on to something happening behind it. Geoff took two more long strides to reach it, swinging the wrench as though he was about to chop a log. He had hoped to crush its head with the attack but had misjudged his timing, expecting the thing to come down the bank a few steps towards him. The wrench narrowly missed, and Geoff buried it into the damp soil at the Romero's feet.

'Fuck.' he grunted.

He knew what would come next. He had put a good deal of force into that swing and was bent forward. The Romeros were dumb, slow, and by and large just annoying when not in large groups, but when it came to feeding time they became very quick with their biting and grabbing. They were strong too, once they gipped an arm or leg the only way that hold was going to loosen was if the hand doing the gripping was separated from its host.

Geoff let go of the wrench as agility and freedom of movement were the key factors here. Tugging a weighty bastard like 'The Fucker' from the ground carried with it risks. But, despite all their strength and speed, when close up and personal the Romeros were very predictable. Geoff straightened up as fast as he could and, as he had anticipated, the top of his head caught the jaw of the Romero as it loomed over his, about to grasp his shoulders and take a bite.

Its teeth flew out and blood and the strange thick mucus they produced sprayed into the air. Geoff took a step back, careful to allow for the incline and reached for his machete. The thing continued to grab at empty air until it realised that its prey had moved. As it lurched forwards Geoff swung the machete, aiming for its neck. The blade, almost surgically sharp, sliced through the Romero's windpipe, but not deep enough to engage with its spinal column. The thing continued to totter forwards, the gap Geoff had created in its neck opening and closing as dark blood and mucus pumped out of it. Geoff quickly leaned forwards and pushed at its chest. While he had a good stance on the embankment the thing did not. Its arms flailed, still trying to grab him even as it fell sprawling to the floor.

Geoff was on it in an instant. He performed two quick strokes with the machete, each removed a grasping hand. The thing attempted to lift itself to a sitting position, the cut in its neck horribly wide, and stretching as the weight of its head forced the skin to tear further. Confident, Geoff moved a step nearer and swung again, this time the blow was true, and the Romero's head was severed. It dropped to the

14

floor and rolled and bounced to the bottom of the embankment, coming to a rest at Bevvo's feet.

'Fucking hell mate. You made a meal of that one.' Bevvo said, grinning.

'Thanks for the fucking help.' Geoff retorted. 'Sarcastic bastard.'

Bevvo chuckled and began to make his way up the embankment.

They moved low and quiet until they were next to the concrete wall running around the ground floor of the car park, then ducked down behind it.

Geoff lifted his eyes above the wall to get a look inside, then slowly lowered himself. The Deads picked up on fast movements far easier than calm deliberate actions.

'Nothing.' He said, quietly.

Bevvo nodded. 'Worth taking a peek around the corner?'

Geoff shook his head. 'No. We stick to the plan.'

'Right.' Bevvo replied, as Geoff retrieved his wrench.

With the The Fucker tightly strapped to his back he nodded to Bevvo. Obligingly Bevvo interlaced his fingers and offered his clasped hands for Geoff's foot. Geoff checked his backpack and weapons were secure once more, then stepped a booted foot into Bevvo's manual lift.

CAR PARK LEVEL 1

Geoff eased over the wall, and as the other side was a shorter drop he was able to swing down onto his feet, crouched. He took another, longer look around the gloom of the car park level. Still nothing stirred. The groaning, humming sound of Deads could be heard, as it bounced off the buildings outside, but that was the only thing he could detect of them. It was still and silent here.

A few cars were parked in the bays, some at odd angles, a couple buried into the backs of others. When it had happened, this place would have been a scene of panic. Geoff committed this information to his mental evaluation of how it had all begun here. He would need more data, but this was a good indication that it had happened very quickly, and during the daytime in this town. In many places the car parks were empty, people had time to move out, or it had been at night and only a few vehicles would be parked. You could learn a lot from places like this if you knew how to look at them. It must have been just as things had begun to get better. Or there would have been less vehicles, less shoppers.

Bevvo's hands appeared on the top of the wall. Geoff rose and helped to haul him over. Once Bevvo had his feet safely planted on the floor Geoff pointed towards the far end of the car park.

'Fast and low. If it goes South, we back up and exit right here. Same thing on each level, if we have to bail we use our grapples to drop to this point on the other side.'

'Works for me.' Bevvo said. It was standard procedure. Repeated only to make sure they were both singing from the same hymn-sheet.

Geoff turned, presenting his backpack to Bevvo who unfastened the coil of rope from it. He did likewise for Geoff. They retrieved their grappling hooks from an easily accessible side pouch which Geoff had stitched on to both packs. The grapples were collapsed into a rod, but with a twist would spring open into a claw. Geoff had traded for them from a militia unit and they had proved to be invaluable. Expertly, they fastened the hooks to their rope and shouldered the coils.

'Ready?' Geoff asked.

'Lead on Gramps." Bevvo replied.

Geoff started off, keeping his head as low as possible while moving with knees bent. It was hard to move well with the backpack, and lately his left knee had begun to give him some trouble. Bevvo's ribbing concerning his age carried more truth to it than he cared to admit.

They cleared the ground level, reaching the far side where there was an exit for vehicles without incident. Bevvo snatched a look outside, a road ran down towards a small junction, on the left, the wall of the shopping centre curved around, following it. On the right was the entrance for vehicles and a little further down he could see what he assumed must be the pedestrian entrance to the car park.

Bevvo raised his hand to make sure he had Geoff's attention. He then pressed his palms together as though praying, then opened them up, signifying a set of double doors he saw recessed into the large wall across the road.

Geoff trotted over.

'Looks like a rear entrance.' Bevvo said.

Geoff looked up. A covered bridge ran from the car park to the shopping centre, and this had been their original destination. He could see Deads wandering up and down inside it. All of them were Romeros from what he could make out.

'Yeah. Looks promising,' Geoff said, looking at the door and then back to the Deads on the bridge.

'Thing is, if one of those guys up there spots us running across they will go fucking nuts and we won't be able to do anything about it.'

Bevvo looked at the Deads up on high. They were stumbling around, looking for all intents and purposes like they hadn't a fucking clue what was going on, but they did press up against the windows occasionally, probably by chance, possibly through instinct, but the fact was they *could* be spotted, and the short cut would end up stirring the whole town into action.

'Alright, we stick with the plan.' Bevvo said.

Geoff nodded and took point again, moving up the ramp to the next level.

CAR PARK LEVEL 2

The disarray on this level was far worse than the fairly orderly scene on the ground floor. A Volvo estate was thoroughly wedged into the back of a Fiat Punto, its own side and rear chewed up by a convertible that was smeared across every panel with dark, old blood.

It was darker in this corner, the light from the open sides of the car park couldn't reach it. Geoff listened carefully. There was movement, but it sounded as though it was above him rather than ahead.

He gestured to Bevvo to come forwards and whispered as he drew near.

'There's something. But not on this floor I think.'

Bevvo nodded.

To their right was an empty space, and next to that an intact Clio. Geoff moved to it and climbed on to the bonnet. The floor of the next level was a foot above his head. Easy to climb up to, rather than walking all the way to the far ramp.

He carefully removed his pack and pushed it through the gap, then pulled himself up and onto the floor. It was tight on the other side. Two vehicles, parked in the spots, had been pushed from behind and right into the barrier. He wriggled beneath their crumpled bumpers until he reached the side, dragging his backpack with him. He saw Bevvo's pack fill the space it left as the lad began to climb up.

Clear of the cars Geoff cautiously stood and looked about, listening for the sound he had heard on the level below. He thought he might have caught it again, a scraping, but it was drowned out as Bevvo scrawled towards him.

'Up this ramp,' Geoff pointed with The Fucker, 'then another one of these and we should be at the bridge.'

As Geoff was talking, Bevvo was taking in the scene of vehicular carnage on this floor, if anything, it was worse again than the previous level.

'This must have been fucking Hell on Earth Gee.'

There had been a fire here. The ceiling was coated with soot. Only a handful of cars were parked up, the rest were meshed into each other, burned out wrecks. There were bones scattered about the floor, clothes, baby seats.

'More terrible than that I think.' Geoff said. He touched Bevvo's arm. 'Come on Bev, we don't have the time for it.'

Bevvo nodded. It still got to him. Even with the fear he faced now, the horror of what had gone before stayed with him.

CAR PARK LEVEL 3

They advanced to the next floor via the ramp and repeated the climb on to the fourth level. With what he had seen so far Geoff was now convinced it had kicked off here during the day, probably at the town's peak shopping period, which was usually a morning. The virus had cut numbers down considerably, but all of this had happened, it seemed, as people were getting better, it had been a cruel twist of fate.

They had begun to return back to some level of normality after weeks of thinking that humanity was doomed. Only to find that they had been correct in the first place.

He could see how it would have gone down. Those on the ground floor, at least the first few, would have been able to exit the car park, but all it would take to turn the place into a demolition derby was one panicked driver on the next level to hit a barrier, another car, a person, or just to brake suddenly. Carnage would quickly follow. Especially if the Deads had appeared on the level.

After climbing through the barrier, they saw the entrance to the bridge they had seen from the car park entrance. A sign reading 'This Way to Shops' was still fixed above the space where double doors would have been. Those now hung to the sides, smashed outwards.

'Does that look suspect to you?' Geoff said.

'Maybe.' Bevvo said, 'Those are automatic doors though, they never open fast enough. Most likely the crowd just burst through them during the panic.'

'Yeah, fair enough.' Geoff replied, pleased that Bevvo's intuition was on form. He hadn't considered that simple explanation, rather he had thought Danny Bees had smashed through the doors and windows. It had been his immediate conclusion that the doors might have been barricaded and overwhelmed, but now that Bevvo had suggested otherwise he could see he had been too paranoid here. There was no sign of a blockade, nothing had been propped up against the doors. But still, it was the monkey who thought the swaying grass was the wind that got eaten by the tiger.

'Ok, now for the fun part.' Geoff said lifting The fucker up as though he were about to step up to first base.

Bevvo took one pick from his belt, deciding to keep a hand free. They moved forwards cautiously, there was very little light ahead. There were no windows in this section, that or they had been covered. Either way it meant dark corners, and dark corners were a fucking waiting to happen.

Fragments of glass from the shattered windows were scattered across the floor and ground underfoot making unwelcome noise. Geoff winced as they trudged across the mess. Two long dead parking ticket machines stood against the wall opposite them, stairs leading up to the next level could be seen just above.

A scraping sound bounced off the walls. Then a light knocking.

'The fuck *is* that?' Bevvo whispered.

'That's what I heard earlier.' Geoff replied.

He signalled for Bevvo to 'Hold Position' and took two even more cautious steps forwards, bringing him to the corner of the stairwell. He peered around.

To his right were three sets of elevator doors, all closed, all banged and dented and smeared with the familiar decoration of old blood. Beyond them and in a recess were two more ticket machines. He followed the wall around. Escalators, going both up and down were visible thanks to the light coming from around the next corner.

'That has to be the windows along the bridge.' He looked again at the escalators descending into pitch black, *'And there's no fucking way on earth I'm going down those bastards.'*

He eased his head around the corner and saw the Deads.

Slowly, quietly he backed away.

'What we got?' Bevvo asked.

'Fuck load.' Geoff replied.

'Oh, not good.'

'No. Not good at all and there's another problem.'

'What's that? Dragons?' He knew that Geoff often understated potential highly dangerous situations.

'One of them has its head stuck in the doors. That's what the noise was, its scraping at them.'

'Brilliant.' Bevvo said. 'Anything else?

'No. Except, if these weren't attracted to whatever drew the others away there's a good chance there will be plenty of others further in.'

'We can handle that.' Bevvo said with genuine confidence.

'We can, if they aren't alerted to us, but if those doors are tough to open we will have a problem.'

'Fair comment.' Bevvo said. 'We also need to have a chat about that unbelievably fortuitous turn of events at some point as well. Do you really think it was blind luck that we arrived just in time for something to draw those fuckers in the Car Park away?'

'Nope.' Geoff replied.

'I thought not.'

'One life threatening situation at a time though eh?' Geoff said, as he slowly slipped his backpack off.

'Ok.' Bevvo said.

'Right. That bridge is fairly long and it narrows about two thirds of the way down. There's Deads pretty much every five feet or so. I reckon we use Freddie to distract them. If he can make it to the two thirds mark we'll have about fifteen seconds while they try to figure out what's going on.'

Geoff unfastened his pack and reached into it.

'Sounds reasonable.' Bevvo said, 'What next?'

'Right, it gets a bit creative here. While they fuck about you are going to spike the guy whose head is stuck in the door. I imagine you will be doing him a favour, he must have the mother of all neck aches right now. Keep him upright, use him as cover and wiggle him about until you can work the door loose.'

'Wiggle him about?' Bevvo said.

'Yeah, you know, as though he's trying to get free. He's probably been trying for three years, shouldn't spook them. I'll be behind you, covered, I'll pull the doors open so we can send Freddie in.'

'Right.' Bevvo replied, doubtful.

'We might get a few come in from beyond the bridge but hopefully they will just fuck off back to the shops after a bit.'

'The guys on the bridge haven't done that, why should the newcomers?'

'Instinct, programming, whatever, these guys were trying to get to the car park when it went down, the others were shopping. They are most likely remembering the last human thoughts they had other than being terrified.'

Bevvo thought about this. It made sense. He had seen plenty of instances of old habits still being displayed in the Deads.

He recalled the Chugger he had encountered a year ago, stood in a town centre not too dissimilar to this one, but far more ravaged.

A momentary lapse of care and attention, which could have easily proven fatal, had seen him duck around the corner of a bank. He came face to face with a Romero. Its face was torn on one side, an eye missing, obviously chewed away. It had been a man in his early twenties he thought, it was always difficult to age the dead. He wore a waterproof jacket that had once been some shade of blue but was now mostly greasy with gore. In its hand it gripped a red plastic container, Bevvo could just about make out the head of a spaniel printed upon it. It was looking amiably at him, its tongue lolling.

The Romero's single eye stared at him, it was wide, surprisingly clear, seeming almost alive. Its mouth stretched back, its lips revealing perfect white teeth set into black gums.

Bevvo reached for his pick, he only had the one back then, but as he did this the thing's other hand shot out and grabbed his arm. Its grip was incredible, squeezing so hard that Bevvo felt nothing in his own hand, and the pick dropped to the floor with a *thunk*.

The thing shook its plastic container.

Up and down.

Twice.

Coins *'ching chinged'* against each other inside it.

Bevvo stared at the thing. It continued to stare back.

It shook its container.

'Ching ching.'

Bevvo blinked. Holding his breath in his throat. He had a one-pound coin in his jeans pocket. It was handy to keep them as many of the smaller supermarkets had shopping trolleys that were chained up. Slipping a pound into the little slot to

25

release the chain was easier and quieter than smashing the thing off.

He pushed his free hand down into his pocket and fished out a coin. Slowly, he lifted it out between his thumb and forefinger.

'*Ching ching.*'

Raisedit over the plastic container with the happy dog still staring at him in the loving, dappy way that only dogs can, and then dropped it into the slot at the top. It made a satisfying *chink* noise as it hit the other coins. The noise that one pound's worth of charitable conscience clearing made.

The Romero released its grip.

It turned and began to move away.

After a few steps it stopped.

'*Ching ching*'

Bevvo walked backwards to the corner he had just emerged from, this time making sure to snatch a quick look with a turn of his head, so as not to blindly run into any more surprises.

He had learned from this, that despite them being mostly alien in their nature the Deads still carried with them traces of their former humanity. And they were just as dumb as the living.

FREDDIE

Geoff pulled out Freddie from his pack. Freddie was a black and white dog. A plastic thing sat on its haunches and holding a golden trumpet at its side. It had big wide eyes, a toothy smile and a clock in its stomach. Underneath were four wheels. It was a wind-up, mobile alarm clock with the most ear grating, ungodly noise both Geoff and Bevvo had heard to date. Well, with one very deadly exception.

Geoff had still not managed to come to terms with it having wheels. Why anyone want an alarm clock that doubled as what he assumed must be a toy was beyond him. But Freddie was worth his weight in gold.

He began to wind each of its keys, the one on the back to start the clock, the one at its side to prepare its little sprung engine.

'Gee.' Bevvo said, as his friend set the little dogs alarm.

'Hm?' Geoff said, distracted.

'I've given it some thought, and I've come to the conclusion that this plan is bollocks mate.'

Geoff looked up at Bevvo with a frown.

'Of course it is. Do you have a better idea?'

Bevvo thought about that for a moment.

'No. Not really.'

'Good. Let's get on with it shall we. Those Deads aren't going to kill themselves.' Geoff said, rising.

Bevvo twirled his ice-pick a couple of times then moved past Geoff to take a look at his target. He peeked around the corner and saw the trapped Romero. It scraped at the buckled doors and worked its jaw.

Bevvo looked back at Geoff, 'Wiggle him about...' he said, and shook his head. 'Unbelievable.'

He moved out from the corner with measured strides bringing him directly in line with the Romero. One fast, solid strike embedded the pick into its forehead. Before its knees could give, and its body slump, Bevvo reached his hand through the narrow gap and held it up by gripping the jacket it wore. It was heavy. He had noticed this before, even the most emaciated Deads seemed to have a weight about them that seemed at odds with their physical state.

He wiggled the Romero.

The doors rattled but didn't give. He looked back and could see Geoff watching with one eye visible from the corner.

Geoff tightened his eyebrows and nodded in a 'Go on son, give it some welly' gesture.

Bevvo rolled his eyes then shook the Romero. The doors rocked but didn't give. He looked again at Geoff, and flicked his eyes up, asking what was happening further down the bridge.

Geoff pursed his lips and shook his head slowly. *'It's fine, all is well, don't worry about a thing,'* was what he was trying to convey, but Bevvo read it as *'Don't look now, but this really bad idea of mine is about to go horribly fucking wrong.'*

Bevvo took a breath and gave the Romero a proper shove. One of the doors dropped from its hinges, the already shattered glass remaining in its frame spilled to the floor creating a cacophony of sound.

Bevvo froze, holding the Romero to him tightly. His eyes slid to Geoff on the corner. Geoff had his wrench at his side, he made a fist, the thumb sticking up from it.

Geoff remained still for a few moments. Watching the activity of the Deads. They often had patterns, they might walk so many feet, then stop, then turn, then walk, then turn around and repeat the cycle. Of all the things Geoff was convinced of the Deads, the Romeros certainly, were creatures of habit.

When he was sure no lifeless eyes were facing his way he moved quickly, but calmly to Bevvo, kneeling behind his legs so as to be obscured by both him and the Romero Bevvo supported.

He placed Freddie onto the floor, brushing away as many fragments of glass as he dared. He wanted to give the little plastic dog as much of a clear path as possible.

'You all right with your new friend up there mate.' Geoff whispered.

'Fuck off.' Bevvo grunted.

Geoff gave him a smile. Pressed a small black button on the back of Freddie and let him go.

The little dog shot off with a light whirr between the legs of Bevvo and the Romero he gripped. Freddie narrowly missed a chunk of glass that would have sent it veering off course and continued to whizz along the vinyl floor towards the Deads, who continued to mill about, oblivious to their colleague being used as a disguise for two men very committed to removing them from the bridge and existence.

After a few feet, the second hand of the clock, recessed in Freddie's belly, swept to 12 and fired up the alarm. A sound that was supposed to be a morning rallying call, a synthesised trumpet, blared out with hellish volume. All heads turned, all eyes, singular and plural followed Freddie's progress past them. Unfathomable cognitive processes acted deep within whatever passed for their minds and the Deads were compelled to follow the little toy.

Geoff watched Freddie's progress through Bevvo's legs.

'Go on Freddie son,' he whispered. It was looking good so far.

When Bevvo heard Freddie's trumpet kick off he looked down to Geoff. They had a routine, it was their Fat Lady Sings, their For Those About to Die, their To Boldly Go, it was shit and it was cheesy and they never failed to share the moment when it was about to go down, because if they were going end their lives in any way at all they wanted it to be with a sense of the ridiculous.

'What are we Gee?' Bevvo said, keeping a tight grip on his Dead.

'We are brothers.' Geoff replied, every time he said this it seemed more real.

'And what do we do when life gives us lemons?' Bevvo continued, taking the Romero onto his shoulder a little more, preparing.

'We make lemonade.' Geoff replied.

Adrenaline was beginning to pump through his system, high octane fuel to power the violence he was about to perform. He stood, making sure he was out of the Deads line of sight by standing side-on behind Bevvo.

'Damn giggidy,' Bevvo said, and began to move forwards, and together, with a conviction that spoke far louder than their controlled whispers, they uttered in tandem,

'We're The Fucking Lemonade Brothers.'

It was tough going for Bevvo, with the Romero's weight threatening to pull him over, but he managed to increase his pace to a trot.

A couple of the Deads looked his way but were completely unfazed by the sight of one of their own apparently running backwards towards them. They returned their attention to the noisy thing that had sped by them.

Freddie had begun to veer to the right after about ten feet and was making his way towards the wall on that side. Slower now, his wound coil almost free of tension.

The Deads began to collect in a jostling rabble above where Freddie stopped in a corner, at the point where the wall of a store reduced the hallway of the bridge by almost a half.

They were confused.

They grabbed at the air and each other. The godawful trumpeting of Freddie filled the air around them. Despite his clockwork engine running down the alarm, powered by four AA batteries would roll on for fifteen minutes or until forcibly stopped.

From behind Bevvo, Geoff plucked his partner's ice-pick from the Romero's forehead.

Bevvo pushed his guest off and to the side. His arms ached, and he waved them in circles twice as he ran, then put his hand behind his shoulder. Geoff placed his pick into it as though they were passing the baton in some kind of murderous relay race. Bevvo pulled out his second pick. With Pinky and Perky prepared it was time to go to work.

Geoff broke from behind him and pulled forward by increasing his trot to a run.

As one they once again descended on the Deads.

Interlude - Three years earlier

ANGIE

Mrs Angela Winter
Wilmslow

Angie had been unable to keep her food down for five days but it was only now that it was really beginning to make itself apparent to her just how ill she was. The sickness she could deal with, because each time it had been fast, almost efficient. She had eaten her meals, which, after the first time, had been constrained to soup, and within no more than five minutes it was all back up and into the sink. She didn't experience a headache or cramps either, before or afterwards. She didn't feel cold or excessively warm or some alternation of both. All told it was a reasonably mild affliction, but she couldn't find out what was causing it and that was the true worry.

She certainly wasn't pregnant. Geoff had been on active duty for five months now and Prosecco and her small selection of Ann Summers toys had kept her sane while he was away. And of course, all the questions she had asked of herself had been asked by her Doctor when she had seen him on day two of her sickness. This included how she was coping with having a husband off doing something, somewhere, for some reason that involved the Royal Marines.

Despite seeing absolutely no evidence of Flu Doctor Tan advised her that Flu was what she had.

'Stay home, drink plenty of liquids and get plenty of rest.' She had said.

She prescribed Ibroprufen, which Angie could buy from Tesco's at half the price the prescription cost, and that was that.

'Thanks a fucking bunch Doc.' Angie muttered as she left the clinic.

She was grateful her daughter was with her father, the ever fucking blessed 'Jack the Lad' this week. There was a first time for everything she supposed. Jack had taken Penny to Benidorm, with him and his wife, the fat arsed bitch he had met, allegedly at a friend's party, after they had split. It had been eight years, and Angie was sure she should really be over it by now, but it still rankled. Even though she had met the man she wanted to spend the rest of her life with, the betrayal always hurt.

She had dated on and off since breaking from Jack. Every one of them a wanker. Two married, at least that she knew of. She had given them the elbow as soon as she had found out. One suitor, Martin, had treated her well enough, but was so boring and sexless that she had actually considered fucking his friend, who had been less than subtle about what he would like to get up to with her if she was 'game'.

Angie had decided that she wasn't. She was worth more than to be used as some sort of playtime fuck, and while Martin might be as dull as dishwater at least he didn't mess around on her. He did need new friends though.

What really smarted was that Penny hadn't instantly disliked and rejected fat arse Josie. Jack had wanted to take her away with him and the bitch a couple of years ago, but Angie had firmly shot the idea down.

'She's too young and you barely know Josie,' she had said, whilst not doubting for a second that Jack had known fat arse for quite a time before the split had happened. But of course, he didn't dare bring that up and so she had won the day.

Eight years later the same argument didn't really carry much weight. Penny had said that she would like to go, and Angie didn't want to appear as the bad guy. For all of his faults, and you could fill a football stadium with them, Jack was a good Dad. Penny adored him, and Angie knew how that felt, and perhaps that is what hurt the most. She had also come to realise that it was Jack who had moved on successfully, as had Penny, which meant that perhaps she was actually the bad guy.

Yet, even with all this hurt, anger and frustration with predictable men and their selfish, insensitive attitudes, she had somehow managed to meet one who made everything *just work*.

They had met in the same way that couples had met for hundreds of years, in a bar, pissed. She had been dragged out by Lisa and her crowd of 'live for the moment' friends who worked at the local casino. At only thirty-six she had thought her days of laughter and joy in the company of other women were done.

A Single mum, a teaching job that drove her to put together an Ikea wine rack (hadn't that been fun), and no permanent man on the horizon. Lisa and all her colleagues were under twenty-five and filled with the thrill of life and youth, and yet she had found it easy to be in their company.

They all complimented her on her looks, something she totally understood was in the hands of her genetics and so didn't get all hooked up on it. She liked to dress well and was conscious of her long hair being clean and well-conditioned, she treated herself to the occasional manicure, but not regularly, certainly not weekly like some of them.

When she had first noticed Geoff, the broad, bearded man who sat alone in a bar packed with people dancing and singing, she had instantly been drawn to him. He wasn't drinking, although a glass three quarters full of some kind of liquid (she would later discover it was Diet Coke) was in front of him, instead he was scribbling something into a small black book.

She followed her friends deeper into the bar. There was a small dance floor at the far side and they dropped their handbags and danced and sang and tortured the hopeful men who hovered at the edge of the floor.

Angie was surprised to see the man at the bar still sat there, writing, when she went to the toilet about an hour later. She had already drunk enough wine and spirits to make her what she called tipsy but was almost certainly referred to by others as 'smashed.'

The drink emboldened her, and she decided that the man with the black book had to be spoken too. He simply *had* too. Bars were for drinking and dancing, not writing.

She moved through the revellers and plonked herself down on a stool next to him. She leaned in, not so dizzy that she lost her balance just yet, but still her hand found his arm for support. She instantly felt a thick, strong bicep under the loose, boring jacket he wore.

'What'cha doing?' she asked, her words a little washy.

The bearded man who would, from that evening on would be 'her Geoff' turned to her, took a long look at the attractive, clearly drunk woman who had gripped his arm, and smiled.

Angie felt her heart flutter. She didn't believe in love at first sight because she had never witnessed it. So what was happening to her right now had no real

35

explanation other than Prosecco, Sambuca and Vodka in action.

For his part, Geoff was wholly concerned that this unbelievably beautiful woman was so drunk that she probably thought he might be her father.

'I'm just writing.' he said, because small talk with attractive women wasn't in his skill set.

Angie smiled. Geoff's breath became shallow. He thought she had the kind of smile that could start wars.

'You a writer?' she asked, 'like Stephen King?'

Geoff laughed a little, 'God no. I just... I write about where I've been. Like a travelogue.'

'Oh.' Angie said, not disappointed, more curious.

'Where've you been?'

'All over.' Geoff said.

'Nice.' Angie replied smiling more broadly. 'Listen Stephen King, I really need to visit the little girls room...' she said, then appeared to think for a moment, then added, 'for a piss.'

Geoff blinked. And realised that he was utterly in love with this spectacularly drunk woman.

'Ok.' he said.

'But I'm going to come back and then you have to tell me all about your holidays, and whether you have your own place and are prepared to take advantage of a lady who has had too much to drink... because I'd really like you to.'

'I'm afraid I can't do that er...'

'Angie.' She said and extended her hand.

Geoff took it and felt the warmth of her skin radiate through his body.

'Angie, Geoff,' he said, then added, 'Angie, I can't do that because you probably aren't who you really are right now, and I think I'd much rather meet the real you and see how that worked out.'

36

Geoff knew he was waving goodbye to what might have been an incredible evening of sex without strings, but it would have also been one without responsibility, at least for him.

He wasn't a bad looking bloke, he knew this, but he had ten years on this girl at least, he was no Brad Pitt or Chris Hemsworth or whoever hell it was making women's hearts skip these days, but whatever happened tonight wouldn't last past her sobering up and he didn't want her regret on his conscience.

Angie stared at him and frowned. She poked his bicep with a finger. Geoff looked at the finger and mirrored her frown. Angie poked him again.

'What are you doing?' he asked.

'Just checking.' she said.

'Checking what?'

'If I'm so pissed that I've imagined a gentleman has appeared from somewhere.'

Geoff laughed. 'I'm very real, honestly. I just… well I just wouldn't want to be a bad guy.'

'Are you a good guy?' Angie asked.

Geoff stopped smiling. He was still caught in this woman's beauty and charisma, but she had asked a question he had been asking himself a good deal lately.

'I think I am,' he said, 'but sometimes I wonder.'

Angie stared at him. Hard.

'Wait there Geoff.' she said, swinging her legs off the stool and standing. 'I'm going to the ladies, and then we'll see if you are.'

Fifteen minutes later she left the bar with Geoff. She took him to her place and they kissed, and kissed and kissed, but Geoff wouldn't allow it to go any further. Instead, he said sweet and wonderful words to her that she would never be able to recall, lay her down on the sofa and covered her with his jacket as she quickly drifted into sleep. He scribbled his number on a page from his book and left it on the coffee table.

She called him at 8am the next morning despite the mother of all hangovers.

Angie had been unable to keep down any flavour of soup. She had tried Chicken, Beef, Vegetable and her favourite, Tomato. Fluids were all right, so long as they were water, or coffee and tea. But no milk. She took her coffee black but liked a splash of milk in her tea, but even that had proven to be something to avoid. At first, this led her to believe that she had developed some sort of lactose intolerance, but further experiments with totally milk free products had quickly ruled this out.

She conducted further trials with her diet after booking a new visit with Doctor Tan, and this resulted in being told by an abrupt receptionist that the soonest she could see her was in three days. The receptionist sniped that she was too busy to even Skype the appointment.

Fruit juice, fizzy drinks and smoothies all set her off, but she had at least found one thing she could keep down that offered at least a little sustenance. Her next door but one neighbour Richard, a sweet old guy in his eighties, always brought around vegetables he grew on his allotment. Angie cut his hair in return, something she had learned when in college, trimming and tidying the wispy strands that remained on his ageing head.

She always cut Geoff's hair and he always complained she had given him a 'Lionel Blair cut.'

She wished he was here, she always wished he was here, but now more than ever. He had called a week

38

ago and said he was done with his duty and would be coming home soon, but that couldn't call again until he was back in the UK. That seemed like a whole other century ago.

She tried the fresh veg, starting with carrots and after ten minutes of not bringing them back up moved on to the parsnips and lettuce. A further ten minutes later she had still not been sick. Angie devoured the remaining vegetables.

She took whatever Richard was prepared to let go of his remaining crop and insisted he take payment for them as well as a promise of cutting his hair as soon as he felt he needed it done. She then blended, boiled and grilled the various plants to vary her newly acquired vegetarian diet, freezing what she didn't immediately consume. Frying them was out though. Fat, and even synthetic cooking oil were guaranteed to return anything cooked in them.

On the Wednesday of her second week of the sickness she had tried to eat carrots from a tin, uncooked, but they had launched themselves back up, as had happened previously. She defrosted a few of Richard's carrots, fresh other than their week in the freezer, and digested them without issue.

She called Doctor Tan's surgery to confirm her appointment was good for today and to relate the information she had about her diet, but there was only a recorded message stating that the surgery was closed due to illness.

It was the same day Jack called from Benidorm to tell her that he, Fat Arse and Penny were all sick.

BEVVO

Andrew Bevington
City Centre, Manchester

Bevvo was late. A glance at his dashboard while waiting at the third set of red lights he had hit, staring in frustration at the illuminated clock relentlessly counting the minutes past nine, while at the same time counting down to his impending doom, told how late he already was for work.

He had woken in good time, much earlier than normal in fact. The weather had been dry and warm over the past two weeks, and it appeared that June was finally turning into a summer month for England.

The sun had begun to rise into a clear sky and as he had woken early Bevvo made the decision to be up and out, jogging across the park-land near to his home before the alarm clock performed its duty.

On his return he showered, shaved and took a bowl of Cornflakes for breakfast, with a glass of orange juice to wash them down. He checked his iPad for any diary events he may have forgotten. It was Dad's birthday in three days, he was playing Roger in Accounts at Badminton tomorrow evening and he was due a check-up with his Dentist on Friday.

Breakfast finished, and diary checked, Bevvo inserted the iPad into its slip-case, grabbed his car keys from the table and headed for the door. As he reached for the handle a pain gripped his stomach which bent him double. He let out a short gasp before his teeth clenched with the agony as the same time pain, like hot knives driving through his guts, stabbed at him again, forcing him to his knees. Bevvo opened his mouth to breathe, but before he could suck in air a shower of orange and brown vomit forced its way out him splashing across the base of the door and carpet.

Tears dripped from his eyes. The initial flow of barely digested breakfast was followed by two shorter lurches producing only throat stinging bile. He dry-heaved a few times, and then his stomach abruptly calmed.

He stood and wiped his eyes. Some of the vomit had splashed on to the knees of his trousers and a string of saliva hung from his chin, dribbling onto his shirt. He would certainly have to change his clothes and decided to take another shower.

After his second total body cleansing of the morning, and other than a mild sting from the acrid bile that had scorched his throat Bevvo felt fine. He retched a little as he took a sponge and soapy water to the remains of his breakfast but powered through to get the job done.

Leaving a milk-based vomitus on his carpet was never going to end well, and even more so in the warm weather so it had to be dealt with, but his main concern was that the whole episode had easily added thirty minutes to his journey time. All he needed now was to be caught up in the rush hour traffic, which he usually managed to avoid with his early rise, to create a perfect storm of a fucked-up morning.

The rush hour traffic waited for him.

It was precisely ten minutes past ten when he briskly crossed the main entrance to Veidt Electrotech PLC. His manager Tris Patel, a smart and dangerously ambitious man was stood by the reception desk and to Bevvo's surprise looked genuinely pleased to see him.

'Bevvo! Thank fuck.' Tris called as he walked quickly towards his employee.

'I'm really sorry I'm late Tris, I've been...' Bevvo started, but Tris cut in as he put his arm around his employee's shoulder in unusually comradely fashion.

'Doesn't fucking matter mate.' Tris said and guided him to the lift.

As they passed the reception desk Bevvo noticed it was unmanned. Cathy was usually there, and if for some reason she was away Debs would take her place. There was no sign of either.

'Bevvo, I've got seven of my fucking guys off the floor.'

'Seven?' Bevvo almost stopped walking.

Tris swore a lot, he used the F word like punctuation, but Bevvo noted that today his profanity usage was off the scale.

'I shit you not mate, I shit you not. Frank, Dobbsy, Melanie, John B *and* John G, Tracy Tits and Fitzy, all off. All sick.'

'Wow.' Bevvo replied, his surprise genuine.

He wanted to explain that he had been sick too, but Tris pressed them on to the lift and kept talking. Tris tended to talk a lot generally. He talked, and swore, and made Veidt a metric fuck-ton of money.

At twenty-three Bevvo knew he was doing well. He was climbing the ladder, impressing the right people, and keeping on the right side of ambitious douche bags like Tris was important.

'Cathy and Debs are both off. Debs ain't ill but her little girls fucking... I don't know, sick... whatever.'

They reached the lift and Tris jabbed the button. The doors immediately opened and they stepped in.

'What about Tony Preece? He was off ill last week, is he back? Bevvo asked.

'Nah. Tony ain't. His wife called yesterday. Cunt's on fluids or something, proper ill.'

'Jesus,' Bevvo said. 'So what do we have? Three guys and me?'

Up to now Bevvo had still been worried about his lateness but he could see that this was the last thing on Tris's mind. With over half his team off the floor Tris's end of day figures were going to take a major shit.

'Can we bring some down from floor six?' Bevvo asked.

'I tried that. They are in the same boat. Four of their people are a no-show, including The Moose.'

'Fuck! The Moose is a no-show?'

Bevvo's shock was again genuine. The Moose was Marvin Mellancamp, the highest score-card keeper in the company. He took one holiday per year, always a three-week stay in Bermuda, and had never had a day off sick in all of his time at Veidt PLC. Time which currently stood at fifteen years.

There were rumours that The Moose had actually bought the island he holidayed on.

'The fucking Moose is a no show.' Tris repeated, shaking his head. 'Some kind of bug from the looks of it. I hope it's not fucking swine flu or some other shit like that.'

Bevvo nodded gravely. He hoped so too. Because if they were all sick and he had been sick it didn't take House MD to figure out it was probably the same thing.

The lift door opened and the two walked out onto floor five of the Veidt building. Six pairs of eyes looked up at him from their monitors. Later he would discover that all of them, including Tris, had been sick that morning.

RETURN TO MAIN FEATURE

Potteries Shopping Centre
Hanley

Six Romero's stood over Freddie, staring down at the plastic toy in a state of what could only be considered bewilderment. Eight others had not been so taken by the noisy clock and had lost interest now that there was already a crowd around it. Geoff and Bevvo went to work on these first.

Geoff made his first swing with The Fucker, piercing and crushing the face of a Romero, who had turned just a moment before impact. Its single eye obliterated as a nail passed through it at an oblique angle. Its tight skin tore apart down the length of its nose and its skull shattered like an eggshell.

He quickly levered The Fucker's spikes out of the ruined head and immediately brought the weapon's bloody business end up and under the jaw of the Dead immediately behind. The Romero's jaw, palate and most of its nose remained enmeshed within the spikes of the wrench until the impact of its return journey, down upon the top of the things head, made the gory detritus fly off in a bloody splat.

Bevvo took out two more Deads on the right with his picks. They were cleaner, more efficient kills. Geoff was a messy bastard for sure.

Bevvo continued through them, his side was always the right side, Geoff took the left. Anything in between was fair game.

An off-target swing caught one of the Dead's in the neck and Bevvo had to compensate by moving in a little closer to Geoff. The Fucker required big swings to give it the momentum it needed to end a Dead in one hit, so Bevvo made sure he could see where his partner was pitching the damn thing. He

45

didn't fancy one of those gore-coated nails tearing his skin open.

With the few wandering Romeros dispatched, both switched to their machetes, leaving their previous weapons buried in their last victim and thereby avoiding any clatter that might be made as they hit the floor.

The machetes gave them the option of taking off limbs, which was handy when heads were not readily available. As the Romero's huddled over Freddie, staring down at the floor, they had to be disabled and then dispatched and quickly.

Arms were the easiest to sever, and without them the Romero's were just walking pinball bumpers. Geoff and Bevvo began to hack at those closest to them. Some Deads could be noisy so it was important to work fast. Once again Bevvo worked the right side and Geoff the left as they butchered their way into the crowd. Where arms were not readily available they struck at legs, always the lower half where the chances of cutting the limb clean off was strongest.

In under a minute the crowd became a pile. The Deads snapped their teeth ferociously at the air, at each other, and where Geoff and Bevvo had removed their arms they rocked and shuddered their shoulders. Those without a lower leg or two attempted to crawl from the bloody mass but were quickly dispatched with fierce blows from the machetes. No word was spoken by either man. They went about their bloody work with cold efficiency.

When it was done, after each Dead had received at least one extra blow to the head if one remained, Geoff pulled away three of the slaughtered creatures to reveal Freddie. The little plastic dog was covered in blood and dark mucus. Geoff pulled a handkerchief from his pocket and retrieved their little companion, he could handle the blood, but he didn't like to touch the vile mucus.

'He ok?' Bevvo asked, wiping flecks of gore from his face, careful not to get it near his eyes.

'He'll need a good clean.' Geoff said, stepping away from the hill of corpses, 'but yeah, he's fine.'

Throughout the assault they had kept a wary eye on the entrance to the bridge. It clearly opened up directly into the shopping area on the first floor and there was a very real danger that a Dead might have wandered by and seen the melee. From the looks of it thought, they had been fortunate, nothing had come by.

Geoff's breathing was heavy. Swinging the wrench was hard, but the fast sweeps of the machete really worked him. Bevvo had worked up a sweat too but appeared more relaxed and still primed for action.

'OK, let's get a look at what we have.' Geoff said, he took a deeper breath and moved to the wall on their right, then slid along slowly until he could see into the retail area. Bevvo did the same thing on the opposite wall so that they had a view of each side.

Bevvo could see five Romero's. They were shuffling along the outside of a small café situated in the middle of an open area. One, a female, waited at the counter as though expecting to be served a Cappuccino and a muffin. She might have been standing there for three years. Bevvo mused that if it was anything like the café near where he once worked, she probably had. He held up a hand, five fingers splayed. He made a face, looking gormless.

Geoff wasn't amused. He understood that Bevvo was indicating that there were five Romero's, but their signal for them was a closed fist. It was the easiest gesture to show and therefore the one to use for the most prevalent type of Dead. He scowled.

Bevvo dropped his shoulders and sighed. He put his hand forwards and clenched it into a fist. He then made the universal 'wanker' sign with it.

Geoff ignored him and took in his own area. The customer walkway where he stood went further back than on Bevvo's side. From here he could make out an elevator, one with glass panels all around. He couldn't see through the glass however as it was smeared from ceiling to floor with blood.

Of great interest to him was an Information Bureau, just ahead. A circular construction inside of which there would be lots of details about all of the shops in the centre. The problem was that there were easily twenty Deads that he could see immediately, and he had no idea how many would be around corners.

He pushed a fist forward, flashed five, ten, fifteen, twenty fingers, then wavered a flat hand, *fuck knows how many more.*'

Bevvo nodded. They had to go right. Even the slow-moving Romero's were too much to handle in that quantity, not least of all would be the physical energy it would require to chop at each one of them never mind how many more would be drawn to the scene.

Geoff slid back a little then crossed to join Bevvo, then pointed, 'There's an information booth just to the left.'

'And twenty dickheads around it? Forget it Gee.' Bevvo replied. He knew full well that Geoff's statement was in fact a proposition.

'We could pick up maps, and stuff on this whole town from right there. There could be all sorts of shit around here we might never know about.'

'Nope.' Bevvo replied. 'Fuck that.'

48

Geoff shook his head. 'Makes me sad to see the way a simple apocalypse has brought down the aspirations of the youth of today.'

'Arsehole.' Bevvo replied.

He edged forward a little, took in another sweep of the centre then slid back. 'Right, definitely five in the immediate area. There's a little café, roped off, tables and chairs, a lot tipped over, usual scene of an attack from back then.

'You sure it's just Romeros?' Geoff asked.

'As sure as I can be without a longer look. No one looking twitchy.' Bevvo replied.

'Fair enough. How's their spacing?' Geoff said.

Bevvo switched places, 'Take a look, pretty bunched up.'

Geoff slid along and observed the Deads as long as he dared. They were in pretty good shape, their clothes, while blood soaked, were intact. Two of them were women, one at the café's serving area, and one sliding her face along the window of W.H Smith. Both had long hair hanging down over their shoulders which had somehow avoided becoming matted with the blood that had once spilled from their torn faces.

One of the Dead's had the uniform of a member of the centre's security staff. A formerly white shirt and pale blue waistcoat, black trousers and shoes. His neck had been ripped open at the side. He stood very still, his hands clasped behind his back staring at the Dead waiting for her Cappuccino. That was some weird shit. The others meandered along the store fronts occasionally looking into the windows.

Most of the large glass panes were intact. Security strength glass was tough to break without some real effort, so it wasn't surprising to him that many would still be in place, but it was unusual to see so many in good order. Geoff looked about the floor.

There were pools of dried blood, smears and trails everywhere. But no bodies. There wasn't a single desiccating corpse or writhing disabled torso in sight.

'*Odd.*' Geoff thought.

It wasn't alien pods in the corner while you slept odd, or Donald Trump's hair odd, but it was certainly not the norm.

'What d'you think?' Bevvo said, as Geoff eased back. His partner didn't reply.

'Gee?' Bevvo said, concerned now.

'Something not right here.' Geoff replied, more quietly than was needed, even in this place.

Bevvo had just about caught the statement, 'Not right how?'

'It's too clean.' Geoff replied.

'Too *clean*?' Bevvo said, a little amazed. 'Are you serious, it's like Dexter's shopping trip out there.'

'I agree.' Geoff said. 'Dexter always cleared away his victims.'

Bevvo's eyebrows knotted together, then his eyes widened. He switched places again and took another look. He then moved back to the other wall and scanned all of the observable first floor. He returned to Geoff.

'No bodies.' he said.

'No bodies.' Geoff agreed.

There were always bodies. When the blood of their victims cooled the Deads left them alone. They moved on to find other warm creatures to feast upon. Those who had suffered a bite, or even a large amount of trauma but had the use of their legs, would rise and join their attackers. But, there were many who were devoured almost wholesale before their corpses became unpalatable.

The remains were seen everywhere. Animals wouldn't feed on them. Even rats. Anything the Deads contaminated with their foulness was reviled by the living and the partly consumed lay where they had fallen and turned to a blackened, evil smelling carcass. They were everywhere, and yet here there were none.

TREASURE

A feeling Geoff had experienced many times while on active duty began to rise within him. It started in the small of his back, like a dull ache. The feeling, the ache, would elongate, and become a line of doubt running up his spine and into the very base of his thoughts. It came when things were very wrong but couldn't be seen.

He had never been a superstitious man, certainly not religious, but events leading up to his return from Afghanistan, his final tour he supposed, had made him question what might exist beyond what he thought of as the real world.

There had always been horrors in the shadows, but since they had emerged into the daylight he learned not to ignore warnings that he once considered as fanciful as the idea of the dead walking the earth.

'What d'you think?' Bevvo asked, unsure of where this placed them with regards to the plan.

They were partners, equals. Geoff never tried to claim any kind of leadership or dictate their path but Bevvo respected his friend's wisdom and experience. At times like this he needed to be given a direction and he trusted Geoff to make the right call.

'We're in,' Geoff said, 'the numbers aren't insurmountable, and this place looks like a goldmine.'

He looked at the floor, clearly running the options through his mind, 'something is... not quite right here, certainly. The Deads being distracted when we arrived, no bodies…' his head nodded a little. '…but we are in good shape, we have a clear exit at the moment and I don't see any problem getting back to it right now.'

'We keep going?' Bevvo said, still a question. He needed Geoff to make the decision.

'I think so. We just have to keep our minds open to threats beyond these dumb fuckers.' Geoff said, eyeing the heap of hacked Deads.

Bevvo nodded. 'Fair enough.'

'I'd really like to check out that information booth too.' Geoff added.

'Fucks sake. You aren't going to let it lie are you?'

'Bev, that right there,' he pointed in the direction of the booth, 'is basically where treasure maps are kept. Long John Silver would have a hard-on for what's in those little spinny displays.'

'Yeah, well that cunt ended up with a hook from chasing treasure all over the place.'

Geoff narrowed his eyes, 'That was Captain Hook from Peter Pan you cock. Long John Silver was missing a leg.'

'Whatever. The point is that I don't fancy getting free parking and a blue badge for the sake of a pamphlet about local artisanal bread manufacture.'

'Knob head.' Geoff replied.

'Just telling it like it is Gee.'

'Look, that desk is around four feet high. None of those pricks have their attention this way. That one, the guard, hasn't taken his eyes off the arse of the Deadette at the counter since we got here. I can shimmy over and grab what we need without them seeing.'

Bevvo smiled at the thought of Geoff shimmying.

'All right grandad,' Bevvo sighed, 'Shimmy away. Fuck it. Go get your treasure maps.'

Bevvo knew Geoff would be an arsehole all day about it if he didn't let him go.

'If it goes south, we exit. Fair?' Geoff said.

'Yeah, yeah, go on, before I change my mind and withdraw my vote.'

Geoff moved to the opposite wall, crouched, and began to slide around the corner, Bevvo moved forwards to gain a better view of each end of the shopping aisle. As Geoff had insisted was the case, the Deads appeared to have their attention elsewhere.

The light inside the centre was far better than he thought it might have been. It was gloomy here but not dark, the roof was ringed all about with windows that still allowed the high sun to flood in. The stores were black inside though, and Bevvo kept a close eye on the recessed entrances where a Romero might be silently staring into its former favourite record store or jewellers.

Geoff moved carefully but with a little more pace than he usually would. He didn't want to be crouched like this any longer than he had too. The pain in his knee was becoming a serious annoyance.

The information booth was a large circular counter with seating inside for two staff members. It appeared empty at the moment, but Geoff was aware that there could be a Dead waiting on the floor, perhaps unable to walk. He didn't fancy leaping over it only to land onto the jaws of an undead tourist information clerk.

As he leaned up against the wooden base of the booth he looked back to the Romeros. They hadn't seen him. He glanced at Bevvo. Bevvo made the 'wanker' gesture at him.

Geoff placed his hands on the booth and slowly lifted himself up. At this point he knew he would be visible to the Deads at both ends of the centre. He

53

moved with exquisite slowness, peered over the counter and saw the floor was just a mess of papers, one of the two chairs inside the pod rested on its back. He lay his chest down on the counter top and eased himself over it.

He paused for a moment.

Listening.

Ready to leap back over the counter should anything approach.

Nothing came.

Geoff slid down the other side of the counter and disappeared from Bevvo's view.

Once settled on the other side Geoff began collecting up pamphlets and pages from the floor, pulling them from around him as he knelt in the middle so as to catch the faint light.

It was a chaotic mix. Leaflets for local companies, bus service timetables, there was a large pile of 'Alton Towers Theme Park 2 4 1' vouchers. He pushed all of these to one side. He was looking for maps of the town, business's that sold equipment they could use as barter, anything that would further increase their chances of walking away from the place with items of value.

He found a fold out street map and with only a brief inspection knew he had hit the jackpot. The glossy sheet looked to have the towns bus routes, taxi rank sites and a legend of stores associated with numbers dotted around the map. He folded it carefully and put it into his inside jacket pocket.

Something made a *click* noise near him, Inside the booth.

He froze.

His eyes darted about in the gloom.

Another noise, this time a *click-click* as something bounced off a shelf and then the floor.

54

An object bounced off his head. It was as though a solitary fat raindrop had landed on him.

'Bevvo.' He thought.

Geoff moved to the edge of the counter with even more caution than had used approaching it. He peered over the top. He could see Bevvo. He guessed he must have been throwing something to get his attention, they kept buttons about them for this kind of thing. His partner slowly raised his forefinger.

'*One.*'

Bevvo walked his fingers across his palm

'*Romero.*'

He rolled a fist over

'*Behind you.*'

He lifted his slightly opened fist to his forehead and bounced it twice.

'*Dick head.*'

Geoff's eyes widened.

He slowly lowered his head and crawled to the opposite side and listened carefully. He could hear the awkward shuffle of worn shoes on the grimy vinyl floor. It was moving past the booth, which was fine, unless its approach triggered the Deads near the café to move in some way, or to turn their lifeless eyes towards the booth. That would not be fine. That would be, to quote his erudite companion, Ultra Shit.

Geoff cautiously followed the shuffled steps on his side of the counter, keeping close to the wooden wall. It was unlikely the Romero would lean over to take a look inside, they didn't have that level of curiosity, but he wasn't prepared to take the chance. He thought it may stop, possibly wheel and head back to where it had wandered from, but it didn't. Clearly this undead was prepared to make a nuisance of itself. Whatever he did he had to keep the thing quiet and decided that had no other option available.

He hoped he had gauged its distance from the counter correctly. He figured it was very close, its body may have even scraped against the wood as it passed. Springing up, Geoff reached over, grabbing the Romero by its neck, and hauled it over the counter in one swift manoeuvre.

Bevvo watched intently, peering from the corner of the wall that concealing him.

'*Ok. I guess that's one way of dealing with it,*' he thought, as the Romero's legs vanished into the booth.

There was a faint scuffling sound. Possibly a grunt. Bevvo looked back to the café, then ahead to where the crowd of Romero's shuffled around each other. All appeared well. Romeros could get noisy when they were attacking, they gurgled, growled and he had even heard them issue gasps of air that sounded like a heavy smokers laugh. It was creepy.

Geoff had to keep the thing silent while he sent it to whatever hell the already dead went to.

It went very quiet.

Bevvo stayed perfectly still.

The last thing Geoff needed was for him to make some sort of commotion while he did his thing.

'*Come on Gramps.*' He thought, barely managing to restrain his desire to rush to the booth. '*It was only one of em… you massive girl…*'

He allowed himself a whisper, 'Come on Gee.'

Geoff's head popped up from the counter. Took a look around. Then dropped down again.

Bevvo closed his eyes and let out the breath he had been holding on too in a long puff.

'*Jesus Christ. One of these days he's going to give me a fucking heart attack.*'

A moment later Geoff reappeared. He slid over the counter and scuttled back to Bevvo.

'Got a map.' He said.

'You took your fucking time with that bozo.' Bevvo snapped.

'You try shoving Alton Towers Vouchers down a zombie's throat without making a noise.'

'Fair enough.' Bevvo replied. As excuses went it had merit.

THREE YEARS EARLIER

BOOTS ON THE GROUND

Captain Geoffrey Winter
Survivors of the Combined Special Forces Group
Manchester Airport

The team deployed from the rear of the Merlin helicopter primed and ready, but for what they didn't know. Only Ollie Petersen, the Merlin's pilot, had spoken on the journey, and purely to advise of the distance to their destination and when they were about to land at Manchester Airport.

Geoff was the first down the ramp, with Corky immediately to his rear. Once he hit the tarmac Corky moved to his side. The others followed, ten more soldiers, their movements identical. Each assumed a crouched firing stance, assault rifles raised.

Captain Geoff Winter and each of his team were fitted out in full tactical gear, each wore a Bergen on his back that looked like it might have mattress solidly squeezed into it. The sight of troops like this would cause concern to locals and enemies wherever they landed in Afghanistan. As they were landing in the heart of England this would likely be considerably more troubling to anyone witnessing them arrive.

It didn't take Geoff's exceptional eye for things that were out of place, to see that nothing here was as it should be. There wasn't a soul to be seen. Aircraft, passenger, cargo and private were parked haphazardly across the whole of the airport's taxi area and black smoke, the kind made when aviation fuel burns in the open air, drifted lazily above the terminal buildings from somewhere behind the windowed structures. Had the conflagration started recently the smoke would be billowing into the sky, Geoff noted.

'Ollie we're on the ground and ready to clear.' He said. The little mic gripping his cheek allowed communication to the chopper and his team for about half a mile.

'Roger that Captain.' Ollie replied.

'You sure I can't persuade you to come with us?' Geoff asked.

'Sorry Captain, but I've got to get to home and see for myself.'

'Yeah.' Geoff replied, 'I understand. Fly safe Ollie, thanks for this bringing us this far.'

'Guys, good luck.' Ollie said, 'Stick with the Captain. He's your best chance of getting through all this.'

A chorus of 'good luck' and 'roger that' buzzed into Ollie's headset from the team.

As the Merlin's ramp began to lift Geoff raised his fist and pointed forwards. He began to move on, scanning for anyone that might cause them harm, his team following with a complimentary level of caution. What they had seen in France was enough to ensure none of them let their vigilance slide. What had happened in Afghanistan had opened their eyes to horrors beyong the scope of the wars and operations they had all taken part in.

All of them, bar himself and Petersen, had been ill and none of the team were from his original unit. What he had now was the last of what he had ascertained to be around two hundred and seventy special forces personnel who had been inserted across the whole of Afghanistan.

As the highest ranking officer he had brought them togehter as an effective force, and as a unit they had fought their way out of a series of nightmares. Now they had finally arrived in England Geoff could see the nightmare wasn't over.

The Merlin was already out of sight as he halted at the side of a luggage vehicle. Cases had spilled from it. It looked as though it might have swerved suddenly throwing them clear. He checked the driver's seat and found it empty.

He could still hear helicopter blades chopping at the air, but it was distant and didn't grow louder. Ollie was well on his way. No jet engines roared and whined. There was no moving air traffic beyond the solitary chopper.

'Corky.' Geoff called.

Tyler Cork, the ginger haired SAS man stepped up to him.

'I don't fancy going through the terminal.' Geoff said, 'I think… around it, head to the car park, pick up vehicles and then we can...'

'We could.' Corky interrupted, 'Or you could come with us.' He didn't disguise his desire for that to be the case.

Geoff shook his head. 'I can't. Like Ollie said, I've got to see for myself.'

Corky nodded, his disappointment obvious.

The SAS man looked unwell, as they all did, and when he caught his reflection in a window Geoff could see the signs of malnutrition appearing. He had declined to eat in front of the team and had found himself cutting down drastically on his food intake, as though in sympathy with their plight.

Corky and the others were tough men, amongst the most the resilient he had ever encountered, and he had walked side by side and fought against some of the best trained and highly motivated individuals in the armed forces, but none of them had eaten for over a week. They were dying, minute by minute their bodies were eating them alive. With what they were up against the irony of this was almost too much for Geoff too bear.

'You haven't been sick Geoff. You could be useful to the lab nerds.' Corky said, his dark ringed eyes implored Geoff to accede to his unspoken petition.

'Once I'm done I'll come to you. I promise. I just need to know.'

'Ok Captain.' Corky said quietly.

Geoff gave a slight nod. He hadn't been sick, not at all, not even as Ollie had been. The pilot had informed him of being unable to keep anything down for about eight days, then he had found that he could stomach chocolate and nothing else, despite trying a banquet of varied meals. For a week Ollie had eaten nothing but Cadbury's Milk Chocolate Family Size bars. He explained to Geoff that it had been the pure lust to taste something other than sugar and cocoa that had driven him to drain a bowl of soup, presented to him by an Afghan local, and he had kept it down. From then on he had been able to eat and digest food properly. It appeared that whatever had affected him was now either gone or retreating.

Geoff had heard of only two other people who had experienced a similar situation. Everybody else was either dead or dying of starvation, or worse. Far worse. But, it could be that the virus, or whatever the fuck it was, had ended. He had to get them all to safety and then they could experiment more with their foods.

They moved across the tarmac, having to cross under a half-dozen passenger jets. Suitcases and backpacks were strewn all about the place, the luggage vehicle had clearly been only the tip of the iceberg. He spied a mobile phone lying face up, its screen black. It reminded him to check his own as soon as they were clear of open spaces.

He halted the team as they reached the corner of the terminal building. He had become accustomed to moving in short bursts, so he could check ahead for possible hostiles, and to give his tired team a moment to catch their breath. From the outside they looked like instant death for anything that threatened to get in their way, but their health was waning fast. They were weak, tired easily, and had become pale. Some of them had visible patches of sore skin that stood out against their pallid complexions.

Geoff still barely knew them. They had come together only through their training. Each man the sole survivor of their unit, each had fought their way back to the most central headquarters in Afghanistan. They had arrived only to find it wholly abandoned by the living but fully occupied by the dead.

'Everyone good?' Geoff asked. Down the line each man nodded.

He looked around the corner, observed all he dared, then pulled back around.

'Fuck.'

'We dancing?' Corky asked.

'Yeah. There's fucking dozens of them.'

'Any of the bad ones?' Corky asked, hoping against hope that his new Captain would tell him no.

'I think so. At least four I think, but possibly more. There's a whole bunch that could have more hidden amongst them.'

'Why the fuck are they here?' Corky said, bitterly.

'People I guess.' Geoff replied,' Lots of people at an airport day or night.'

The first thing he had noticed about the Deads was they tended to collect at places where the living might have once been in number.

Corky shook his head. 'Oh man. This is so fucked.'

'Yes, it is.' Geoff agreed. 'Do you think you could make it through them? If I could take down the fast ones?'

'I think so.' Corky said.

His stomach cramps had subsided on the Merlin and he felt as though he would be good for a while. 'But I'm not sure about the others.'

Geoff looked down the line. His instinct told him that Corky was right.

'Plus,' Corky added, 'if we fire these guns we are likely to bring even more to the show.'

Geoff nodded. The guns which had for so long been the very signature of conclusive violence he could bring to a situation were now mostly a handicap. They were still highly effective against the living, but usually nothing more than an inconvenience to the dead, and it was as though the sound called to them. After all, it took the living to make a gunshot, and so they came.

'We only need to get to the cars. We're not planning on sticking around so the extra Deads won't matter if they aren't close.' Geoff said.

'Yeah, fair enough, but we have to find vehicles we can start, so they'll need to be old unless the keys are in the ignition. And those fast fuckers? If we can't take them out of the game, we aren't going to last long enough to start shopping for a twenty-year-old Ford Escort.'

One of the men grunted. Geoff and Corky looked towards him. It was Phillipe, twenty-five years old, a member of the French Special Forces Brigade. He balanced on his heels, back against the wall, knees bent. His arms were wrapped around his stomach.

'Phillipe, est-ce que vous allez bien?' Geoff asked, subconsciously cursing his lousy French language skills.

'Oui, Capitaine,' Phillipe said, in a strained voice, 'juste une crampe.'

Geoff exchanged a grim look with Corky. The Lancashire man was right, they would bring every Dead in the area to them if the guns were used, but what other options were there? Just running from the chopper to this end of the terminal had been tough on them, if they cramped up while running, as Phillipe was doing now, they would be taken down.

Geoff looked about the runway and taxi area for an answer, and after a moment dropped a hand on Corky's shoulder.

'All right, I think I have a way through those fucks.' He signalled for the team to *hold position* and to *keep em peeled,* then turned to Corky.

'Give me ten minutes, if I'm gone any longer I want you to risk your life and the lives of everyone else to come and find me.'

'Understood.' Corky replied.

He got it, they were to progress as best they could without him. In just a few weeks he had learned to appreciate that Captain Winter had a hell of a sense of humour regardless of the situation.

Geoff moved off, jogging under the bellies of the jets and back the way they had come from the chopper. In just under eight minutes he returned with the vehicle that was to get them through the massing Deads. The lads looked at it with surprise and measured doubt.

'All aboard.' Geoff called from the luggage vehicle.

Corky and the team approached the vehicle. A simple electric powered luggage cart hauling five canvas-walled carriages.

'No chance this is going to be faster than those runners Captain.' Corky said. 'Even if we uncouple the carriages.'

'We aren't going to uncouple the carriages, and we only need to move without stopping.' Geoff replied, as he climbed down from the seat. 'I'm going to lead them off, you guys are going to hide until we reach the car park. You disembark, hopefully without being seen, and start picking vehicles.'

'Hide where? Inside those?' Corky pointed at the canvas covered carriages.

'Yeah. We'll secure the cases and bags as best we can, use em as a barricade in case of problems. We'll leave a gap on one side so you can bail out.'

Geoff then walked along the line of men, who stood contemplating the idea.

'Two per carriage and I'll need one more up front with me. I need someone who still feels strong enough to fight one of the runners off if it made a grab. He'll also be driving.'

'I'm up front.' Corky said immediately, practically daring anyone to challenge his statement. No one did.

Geoff nodded, then continued back along the line, addressing the lads.

'This is a terrible idea I know, but the fact of the matter is that we need to be mobile. We need to get away from this place. We all know what France has become and the odds are that it's the same here. This pretty much confirms that the United Kingdom has gone to shit.' Geoff waved his hand back at the empty jets, 'and that this is probably everywhere.'

Each man looked uncomfortable but said nothing. Captain Winter had dragged each of them from the jaws of hell over the last few weeks. They were trained to follow men like him, it was in their blood. If he told them to wear dresses they would only ask what shoes would be suitable.

Corky knew that some of them, possibly all of them were going to die. Leaders only talked like this when the situation called for martyrs. But they were dying anyway, and the luggage vehicle at least looked like it might be fun.

'Saddle up boys.' Corky said, and began to direct the team in pairs to the carriages, placing Anders and Shaw into the rear carriage. They were the least prone to dizzy spells and cramps, and Shaw was probably the best marksmen he had ever seen.

Phillipe was paired with Rowley, a baby faced, man with a substantial beard but a head clear of a single hair. He was SAS and spoke fluent French, most of the team had at least two languages available them, and was tremendously strong considering his state at present. Unfortunately, he suffered from stomach cramps frequently and was liable to be incapacitated for a minute or so at a time.

The only non-European was Niemcyzk, a Navy Seal who even now refused to explain why he had been found where he was in Afghanistan, but then Corky had noted that Captain Winter was reticent about explaining his mission over there too. Niemcyzk went into the first cart with Rowley. If the SAS man cramped up he would need the stronger man to haul him up.

Once the men were in position and had created their fragile walls made from holiday luggage, Corky secured the canvas panels on each side. He realised he only knew the first name of the Captain and the French guy, and he didn't actually know the French guys surname. It probably wasn't worth the effort now. He checked his firearms.

'No way this will go quietly.' Corky said, and reconsidered asking the French guy his last name.

THE PLAN

Geoff had been prepared to hot-wire the luggage car but the key had actually been right there, as though the Gods had decided to give him a break, especially as upon seeing the vehicle his first thought was that it might have been left engaged, and the charge in its batteries dissipated. But, the little vehicle whined into action the moment he turned the key and Geoff breathed more easily.

It was possible, he thought, that there might be other vehicles left like this. Keys in the ignition, batteries charged and fuel tanks full. If they could get just one they could get out of the airport and then seek out others once there was less threat. What *others* entailed he hadn't decided yet, but the lads did have a plan of their own and it was at least something to drive them forwards. Soliders worked best with a mission.

Beyond the airport there was the danger of traffic being piled up on the roads. That could be a big problem, especially if they were being followed and the Dead's, both the slow ones and the nightmare runners were very fond of keeping after you.

'*One life-ending scenario at a time Captain.*' Geoff thought.

His order to the men was that no one was to fire from the carriages. If anything attempted to clamber inside it should be dealt with silently and invisibly. Under no circumstances should they make their presence in the carriages known.

Geoff and Corky collected grenades from the team, leaving one for each man for emergency use, they then took their place on the lead vehicle. Corky sat, and took in the cart's spartan controls The luggage car was basically a go-kart.

As Corky familiarised himself with his new ride Geoff checked his weaponry and ammo. He had obtained a long, vicious looking knife in France, it was almost a sword. He slid it into the back of his belt. He would have to be careful with that. It was hard for him to imagine having a more dangerous weapon strapped to his rear. What a fucker that would have to be.

Corky had found a bag of Golf clubs and taken a Nine Iron out, he wedged it behind his seat. Despite being armed to the teeth with military issue guns and explosives, having a rudimentary length of metal with which to smash skulls at his side was comforting.

'What's your handicap?' Geoff asked as he watched Corky push the club behind his seat.

'I'm can't sing.' Corky replied without skipping a beat. Geoff decided there and then that Corky was a man to rely on.

'Ready?' Geoff asked.

Corky turned to face Geoff. 'If they get me, kill me.' He said, as serious as a Doctor delivering a Cancer diagnosis

Geoff nodded gravely.

'If they get me, rescue me at all costs, everyone is expendable. Take me to a top-secret government installation where they have a cure and civilisation has been restored. I don't do hero.' He replied.

Corky smiled and found himself almost laughing, he had to hold it in.

'Yeah, Ok, I'm ready.' He saind, and turned the ignition key. The little electric vehicle shuddered into life and the Deads turned their heads, almost in unison.

The whine of the luggage car was strange to them and so worth investigation. Even those without eyes, of which there were many, birds having snatched them out before they turned, or and their bodies filled with the black goo, observed its approach as only the dead can.

The object and reason of their existence was near, and getting nearer. There was flesh, meat infused with hot blood pumping around and through it. They moved. Limbs which were awkward and heavy carried them on. The prey in turn came towards them. Some lifted their arms and hands if they had them, in anticipation of getting close to the hot flesh. Jaws began to work, moving up and down, preparing.

A low groan rumbled through the crowd. The flesh closed on them and the hunger, which was always present, grew into a sensation so strong that it caused the only pain they could feel. They walked to intercept their prey without guile or tactic.

Some could travel with speed, their legs and arms were more agile, muscles and tendons were still sprung in death as they had been in life, perhaps more so. They ran at the flesh without strain or stress, they could leap and climb and pull the screaming prey down from places where their prey thought they might be safe. Yet like their brothers and sisters shambling behind them they lacked any capacity to dodge or weave, or to seek cover when gunshots began to sound and their own corrupted meat began to spray about them.

'Please don't tell me this is as fast as these fucking things go.' Corky snarled.

The luggage car was moving along the tarmac easily with its five carriages, but at the pace of a light jog.

'Don't worry about it,' Geoff said, 'just keep it pointing in the right direction. Stick with the plan.'

'Fuck me.' Corky muttered.

Geoff snapped his assault rifle to his shoulder. Five figures had broken away from the nearing mob of Deads.

'Here they come.' He said, and began to open fire.

There was no point trying to score a head shot. Although the things appeared to have no inclination to avoid his aim, their feet, beating at the tarmac with terrific speed, created enough sway in their heads to prevent effective targeting.

Geoff selected burst fire, settling for catching their thighs but hoping to hit the knees or below where there was the chance of a round completely disabling them. He sprayed his shots in a narrow cone.

His marksmanship was generally good, and the slow but steady movement of the car worked in his favour. The left leg of the nearest Dead, no more than fifteen feet away when struck, was torn almost completely away. Only a thin strip of skin kept it associated with its owner. The Dead flailed and fell heavily onto its face.

Geoff didn't pause to admire his good work. He switched his sights to the next nearest and began to pepper them with rounds. Two more of the running Deads tumbled to the floor, their legs butchered.

'Two closing Captain.' Corky yelled.

'No shit.' Geoff answered, dropping the assault rifle to the floor and switching to his pistol. He calculated that he wouldn't have time to switch out clips.

'I'll take the left.' Corky said, pulling his own pistol free from its holster.'

'No. Keep this thing straight. I've got this.' Geoff countered.

He jumped down from the luggage car, careful not to tumble, and moved to meet the oncoming Deads.

'What happened to the fucking plan?' Corky shouted after him.
'This is the fucking plan.' Geoff shouted back.

ROPE A DOPE

**Potteries Centre
Hanley**

'So, what's the plan? Rope a Dope?' Bevvo asked, as they eyed the small group of Deads clustered around the Café.
'Yeah, I figure that's where we start.' Geoff pointed to the nearest Romero.
It had probably once been a man in his late fifties, maybe early sixties, he wore a pale grey t-shirt with a pattern picked out in white upon it. The print was mostly obscured by blood which had spilled from his back. When he turned away from them, Geoff and Bevvo could see that the tee hung on by the thicker material of the collar at his neck, the rest had been torn away and the skin and flesh from his back devoured.
Bevvo unfastened the coil of rope from his pack and set about making a loop. Once complete, Geoff took it, he was better at placing the loop than Bevvo, insisting that he had been taught by genuine cowboys.
Bevvo was certain his friend was taking the piss but, the fact was Geoff had a knack with the lasso which eluded him, no matter how much he practiced.
Geoff stepped back a little and began to wind the rope into a spinning circle. He held his position for a while, taking quick peeks around the corner to ensure no Romero was looking their way. Spying his

72

moment, he stepped forwards and let the end of the rope go. It was as good a placement as he could hope to make. The loop of the rope dropped almost at the feet of the Romero. Its gentle rap against the floor alerted the Dead to its presence and it turned slowly to investigate. It still stared ahead, apparently unaware that the noise had come from within an inch of its feet.

Dark, basic instincts advised it to move forwards, to shuffle on in the direction of the interruption. There had been other noises, but they hadn't appeared to be signs of food, nothing to feed its hunger, but the accumulation of them was sufficient for its simple mind to reach a decision. It took an unsteady step, placing its foot directly into the loop.
Geoff quickly, and quietly took the slack, then pulled, hard.
The Romero upturned instantly, like Buster Keaton slipping on a banana. Its wet, naked back made a *SPLAT* noise as it hit the floor and its head cracked. Had it been alive the fracture to its skull might have caused problems, but the Romero only noticed that its perspective on the world had changed, as it looked up at the ceiling. Surprise was not an emotion the Deads were capable of experiencing, but confusion was applied when its raw understanding of the world was disrupted.
As it was being hauled along the floor, Geoff and Bevvo heaving on the rope around the corner, the Romero attempted to stand, not comprehending that it was being prevented from performing that operation by the rope gripping its ankle. As the strange thing was happening to it something close to intense joy filled its thoughts as it rounded the corner and saw the two, radiant, hot-blooded bags of

flesh above it. The eyes it didn't need to see with widened with what could be approximated as delight.

Bevvo slammed a pick into the lassoed Dead's forehead. The Romero shivered and then became utterly inanimate. Looking at it now, it seemed to Bevvo as though it had been dead for a long time. This was often the case, as though the time it should have been properly dead had caught up in that instant and reverted the thing to its natural state.

'One down.' Geoff said, unfastening the rope.

'Four to go.' Bevvo replied.

Geoff took another look around the corner.

'Doesn't look like Undead Harry here caused much of a fuss. Security Guy is still checking out Coffee Chick's ass, and she's still trying to get her skinny de-caff. The other two are checking out PS4 games.'

'I was an XBox man myself,' Bevvo said, looking over his shoulder. 'Better exclusives.'

'Ridiculous.' Geoff replied, contemptuously. 'PS4 pissed all over Xbox.'

'They do say you get more right-wing as you get older.'

'What the fuck...?' Geoff said, thrown by the non-sequitur.

'Too far to rope.' Bevvo said, carrying on his report as though nothing has been mentioned of console games and gaming.

'Yup.' Geoff replied.

'Too close to snipe as well.' Bevvo added.

They both possessed a silencer for their weapons, Geoff had a cumbersome cylinder for the rifle he kept disassembled in a box, and Bevvo for his Beretta, tucked away in his backpack, but they were not truly silent, and somehow the muted shots were still picked up by the Deads. Only humans failed to detect it.

The weapons were secured to prevent them using them rashly, a single shot from a gun was huge draw to the Deads. It was as though they recognised it as a sure sign that humans were abroad, and so they came, almost as though from nowhere, and in large numbers to the source. Guns were only ever to be used as a last resort.

'We just need to take out Security Guy.' Geoff said, 'if we can get him the others will be easy.'

'I'm not sure her backside is going to be enough to keep his attention from us if we move in.' Bevvo said, 'and we can't use Freddie out here, we will end up with all those bastards on the other side wandering over.'

'True fact.' Geoff replied.

He stroked his beard. He hadn't expected to see two such immobile Deads. Normally they strolled around the place, eventually coming within reach of their various traps, but Security Guy and Coffee Chick hadn't moved an inch.

'*Not one inch.*' Geoff thought.

He narrowed his eyes. A thought came to him.

'Bev.'

'What?'

'What if they're already dead.' Geoff asked, only partly a question.

'Of course they're dead.' Bevvo replied.

'No. I mean dead as in dead dead. Dead like nob head here.' Geoff flicked his eyes to the Romero that Bevvo had just spiked. 'They haven't moved even slightly since I first saw them, and we've been pretty busy since then.'

Bevvo took another look. Geoff was right, both Security Guy and Coffee Chick were absolutely stationary.

'That is a bit weird. I've never seen them that still before.'

'Yeah, me either, unless they've been topped.' Geoff said, still scrutinising them.

He could see no obvious sign of head trauma on Security Guy or the woman at the counter, but in her case it could be just as likely that the whole of her face was chewed off as he couldn't see it.

Geoff looked again at the café and its surroundings, taking in the big picture rather than focusing on the little things. He realised he had overlooked the obvious.

'Coffee Chick isn't real,' he said as the answer dawned on him.

'Uh?' Bevvo said, not sure he had heard Geoff correctly.

'She's a dummy, a uh… mannequin. Look.'

He pointed to the displays around the café. There were suits and dresses presented inside wooden display cabinets. 'Summer Season' banners were displayed above them.

'Some clothes store was using that area for advertising a new range or something. I'll bet you ten quid that around the corner we'll find Coffee Chicks boyfriend, or whatever, more mannequins. This one, I don't know, it was probably on the end there, and in the panic got pushed or knocked to where it is now.'

Bevvo considered Geoff's suggestion. Coffee Chick was standing with impeccable grace, her shoulders were straight not slumped, her head didn't bow or indicate her jaw was moving up and down, as it did with Romeros as they ambled around drooling their black mucus.

'Fuck me. You're a proper Sherlock Holmes mate.' Bevvo said. 'What about Security Guy?

76

Geoff now pointed towards the Security man who still observed the perfectly pert backside of the thing at the counter.

'Look at the plate glass behind him, it's not shattered but it is cracked near his head, and I think it's frosted closer in. I'll bet a month's supply of toilet roll something went through that window and into the back of his head. I'll bet it's still there, holding him up.'

'Ooh, that's a stretch Geoff. And by the way you still owe me toilet roll from that Termintor 2 wager.'

Geoff pointedly ignored the last. 'I know it Bev. I just fucking *know* it. That prick has been properly dead since the day this all went off.'

'Ok,' Bevvo said, 'but that would make him the only actual body, other than the ones we created today, on this floor.'

'Yeah.' Geoff agreed, 'and that is still something that bugs me.' He rose from his crouched position, feeling like the situation was coming back into his grip. 'But right now I'll take it that all we have left to deal with is the two happy shoppers behind the café and we can move on.'

'Fair enough. I'll certainly be up for getting past here. Let's see how good your intuition is.'

Bevvo tightened his pack, holstered his ice-pick and performed a final check of the situation at each end of the aisle. The Deads to his left were still milling around but showed no sign of shuffling towards them. To the right, Security Guy and Coffee Chick remained static. The two who were window shopping had moved out of view, shuffling behind the partition created by the café's walls and the clothes store's displays.

'Ok. We're good.' Bevvo said. He stooped and quietly scurried across the aisle towards Security Guy.

Geoff watched, ready to act should he be proven wrong and his dead Deads suddenly became active, but there was no movement from the guard even as Bevvo slid up to its side. He observed intently as his friend peered around the glass frontage the guard appeared to stand against. Bevvo then disappeared into the darkness of the Virgin Media store.

A few moments later he reappeared in the doorway and gave Geoff a thumbs up.

'*Ok*,' Geoff thought, '*here we go.*'

As Bevvo had done, he checked his pack was secure, he didn't want it slipping and falling to the side. When moving stooped or crouched the weight of it could cause him to topple if that happened.

He checked the position of the Deads to the left. They were still oblivious. Meandering through the aisles and into doorways. Pressing faces up to the windows and gazing at the inert electrical supplies and worthless jewellery with an unfathomable longing.

He moved out, skirted around the café on the opposite side to Bevvo. He finally saw the front of Coffee Chick. She was the most perfect woman he had seen in a long time. Her plastic lips were painted a vibrant red and her eyebrows were arched, alluringly drawn. As he slowly edged around the partition of the café he could see his target in the doorway to a GAME store. Its windows were filled with colourful posters of XBox, PS4 and Nintendo games. A large cardboard Pikachu standee declared that you had to 'CATCH EM ALL!'

Geoff thought that having an angry electric furball kicking off wouldn't be much help in here but still thought it could be fun to have one.

The doors to the store were wide open but the Romero only swayed at the entrance. She looked like she might have been a mum once, perhaps she had been up here with her kids. Maybe on the day it had gone down here she had come to buy them some treats. Maybe because they had been so good while they had all been ill. Maybe they hadn't eaten at all, and she thought perhaps she could keep them entertained until they managed to see a doctor, or they started to get better. Perhaps they had died and she had gone fucking crazy.

Geoff shook his head. He had to stop letting his mind run with these kinds of thoughts.

Life had gone on almost as usual for a few weeks when it had begun. A day of disruption when everyone was sick followed by a couple of days of concern as it became common knowledge that the sickness was global. But no one had died from it. At least not at that point. Everyone could miss a few meals and cope well enough.

Adults went to work but children were kept off school. Industry slowed, offices went to half-staff, government remained solid, at least on the surface, and hospitals burst at the seams from the complications of missing a few meals, especially for the elderly and those with already fragile health.

After three weeks it was chaos. You couldn't see a doctor because your doctor was ill, the police couldn't help you because the police were ill, firemen, soldiers, politicians, teachers, celebrities were all unable to keep their food down. And something else had happened, during this period when the sickness had taken hold. When mankind was weakened, but still trying to go about the daily business of civilisation, a plague just as terrible had surfaced. It had taken a while to become apparent, but when it finally hit, it hit hard.

Geoff reckoned that this town must have been attacked suddenly and without warning. It had ended quickly too. One of the things that surprised him was how erratic the infection rate was. He had seen people, healthy people, killed by the Deads and subsequently turn within minutes. Yet, there had been those who had lain still and empty of any kind of life for days, only to suddenly rise and begin walking. There was no rhyme or reason to it.

The mum at the door still had her back to him when he saw Bevvo advance on his Romero. This one had been lightly bouncing against the large glass panes of W.H Smith. He looked old. Probably in his late sixties. He had probably been able to eat normally, or at least manage a food that kept him mobile. Geoff couldn't see the extent of his injuries from here, but the old man's jacket was hanging off his right shoulder and a dark patch indicated a good deal of blood had spilled over it.

As Bevvo moved in Geoff took his The Fucker in hand and followed suit. They struck almost simultaneously. The doorway gave Geoff ample room to swing and he powered the wrench around as though he were striking a baseball. The nails drove deep into the undead woman's skull which in turn crumpled under the force. She dropped to the floor, her weight pulling Geoff forward a little.

Bevvo had to be careful that his attack didn't shatter the window. The Romero was pressed right up to it. He moved in quickly and low, kicked the man's legs from under him and embedded his pick into his head the moment he struck the floor.

Withdrawing the pick he quickly looked around in case there were Deads they hadn't observed from around the corner. Nothing stirred. At least nothing immediately apparent, but there was some sort of noise coming from further ahead.

Geoff came to Bevvo's side.

'All right. Looks good.' He said, also checking for possible Deads secreted in dark corners. 'See any stairs?'

Bevvo shook his head, 'Nope, but there's fucking escalators.'

'Shit.' Geoff said bitterly, 'There must be some stairs.'

'You went to all that trouble to get your little map why don't you check that?'

Geoff silently cursed himself.

'I'm a jackass.'

He took out the map and opened it up as Bevvo looked out for anything coming around the corner they had just come from.

'Fuck.' Geoff said.

'Sup?' Bevvo asked, looking back to him.

'There's stairs but they are through there.' He pointed towards the wide-open entrance to a Debenhams store. Beyond a couple of feet, the store was in total darkness.

'Where? Inside the obvious hole of surprise death and horror? Fuck that.' Bevvo said.

'Fuck that righteously,' Geoff agreed.

'I guess it's the escalators then.'

'I fucking hate escalators.' Geoff said, folding the map and returning it to his pocket. 'I *fucking hate* escalators.'

'It's that or Debenhams mate.' Bevvo said.

He wasn't relishing the prospect of what was about to happen, but it sure beat walking through a pitch-black department store. Torches were a no-go. Dark stayed dark. Light up a Torch and you may as well follow it up with a Ghetto Blaster at full volume for added effect. Deads made a beeline for artificial light and sound. The only thing more likely to get their attention was someone waving and shouting 'I'm over here, come and get me.'

Geoff puffed. 'I suppose so.'
As he was about to start forwards Bevvo placed a hand on his shoulder.
'Mate.'
Geoff turned. 'What?'
'You are right. This place really is a fucking gold mine. Seriously, it looks untouched. I've never seen anywhere like this, have you.'
'No. No I haven't.' Geoff replied.
He glanced around at the stores immediate to them, W.H Smith's, while untidy, books had been knocked from shelves, a dump bin of bargain colouring sets had spilled onto the floor, was practically as it would have been on the day the place went to hell. The Jewellers windows and doors were still in place. They must have locked the doors when it went off, perhaps a security protocol, no one had tried to smash their way in. Gems, rings and necklaces had virtually no value, but a decent timepiece was still desired. One of the window displays was filled with rows of Omega and Rolex wristwatches.
'And that worries me Geoff.' Bevvo said, not scared but clearly concerned. 'Why hasn't anyone done what we are doing? This hasn't been so tough so far. Hell, if we put our minds to it we could probably take on the other side of this floor.'
Geoff nodded. 'Maybe we just got lucky.'
'Right.' Bevvo replied in his most cynical and dismissive tone, 'Cos we're dead lucky aren't we?'
'We survived, didn't we?'
'Didn't we just.' Bevvo replied. 'Didn't we indeed.'
Geoff said no more. He moved off towards the escalators. Thinking only that, considering Bevvo had a good sense of humour, he could be a real fucking killjoy at times.

POLE DANCING

There were two escalators about twenty feet apart. One leading up to their floor the other down to the next, beyond them was a children's play area in the middle of the wide aisle. Neither man had any intention of investigating that.

Geoff looked over the rail protecting customers from the forty-foot drop to the ground floor. He saw a familiar sight. The stairs of the escalator, from top to bottom, writhed with bodies.

'Every fucking time.' Geoff said quietly.

'Pole time?' Bevvo said.

'Pole time.' Geoff repeated.

He turned to allow Bevvo to pull three rods from a long pouch, another that he had fashioned, from the side of the pack. Bevvo then turned his pack to Geoff who did the same. They inserted each rod into another until they both carried a steel spear. Geoff had made them in an engineer's workshop they had found, and they had proved invaluable for dealing with Deads at more than arm's length.

'Up or down?' Geoff asked.

Bevvo looked over the rail. 'Down I say. Seems wrong to walk down the up escalator.'

'Not much of a rebel, are you?' Geoff said.

'Who the fuck I have got left to rebel against?' Bevvo asked.

'Fair comment.' Geoff replied.

They walked to the top of the escalator that would have once borne its pedestrian customers to the lower floor. Many of them were still on it today. Geoff had witnessed this same scene dozens of times and he recalled reading of something similar happening in the second world war. Frightened citizens had run for the safety of shelters in the

84

London Underground, the stairs down to the platforms were steep and sometimes wound around. Someone had fallen, or been pushed, he wasn't sure of the details, but something like one hundred and seventy adults and children had died on the steps. Crushed or suffocated. It seemed an impossible number until you saw what could happen on the escalators. All it took was fear.

Similarly, here, in the panic, someone had fallen, perhaps at the top, perhaps in the middle, possibly even at the bottom. The customers would be casually standing or even briskly trotting down one side as others made way, then there would be the thing that startd it, the panic. Screaming, fighting and ultimately biting and tearing would happen.

A domino effect occurred. People tripping, pushing, falling and sprawling over the metal steps as they performed their automated decline. Eventually the stairs would halt. Some security measure would kick in, but it would be too late.

As more people tried to get to the lower floor those already fallen would be stamped upon or suffocated as the bodies of those above them pressed against their mouths and noses. Some would turn quickly, and begin to chew and rend the skin of anyone around them. They would snatch at the ankles of those trying to step over them and pull them down.

Once the fury was over, when the last customer had fled or been slaughtered, the Deads would try to use the escalators. Their simple minds guiding them without any thought as to why. They would stagger over the bodies of their fellow Dead's until they fell over the side or tumbled to the first floor, adding to whatever injuries they already had.

'I'll go first.' Bevvo said, waking Geoff from his thoughts.

He was about to step aside to let Bevvo through but checked himself. His knee ached. The throbbing from the side of it had become more pronounced. If he fell here he could end up bitten. But if he fell onto Bevvo they could both cop for it.

'No, I'll go.' Geoff said. 'Your eyesight's shit.'

'Oh, cheers mate. Big me up eh?' Bevvo said, feigning hurt feelings.

Geoff held his weapon in front of him as though he were spear fishing. He gingerly placed a foot onto the back of one of the corpses. It didn't move but the his weight upon it caused a Dead underneath to stir. He couldn't see a head to poke with the spear and so took a further step.

Lots of the bodies were genuine corpses, 'proper dead' as Bevvo would say. Geoff could see that many of the heads had been chewed to the spine. Deads rarely ate the head, or at least the brain. They would attack any part of the body at the first strike and once the victim had been subdued they might snack on the face a little, but they usually went for everywhere but the head. He was convinced that this was a part of whatever it was that made up the cognitive systems of these things. That somehow they understood that destroying the brain of their victims could lead to their own demise as their numbers dwindled. Wherever possible Geoff went for the head, and he guessed that the trapped Deads had given in to their cravings and devoured whatever their teeth could get to.

He took a few more steps unmolested but stopped as hand thrust up from the mess of bodies. He peered into the mass and saw a ruined face staring up at him, the hand snatched uselessly at the air. Geoff lifted the spear and drove it down into the things left eye. The hand fell limp.

Behind him Bevvo moved in sync. Treading where Geoff had trod, looking for anything his friend might have missed. It was tough to both maintain balance on the uneven mass of limbs and to keep the spear ready in front of him. One bad step or surprise ankle grab and he could be over the side and smashed on the floor below. Geoff was right, escalators sucked.

Geoff speared two more Deads as he pressed forward. He stopped to look back at Bevvo, just to make sure the lad hadn't silently taken a swan dive over the side, and blinked.

He held up his hand.

'*Stop*'

Bevvo didn't question this. He knew better. He stopped dead in his tracks, one foot on the spiked head of man the other on the gore streaked dress of a young woman. He wobbled a little.

Geoff's eyes flicked up and to the right and Bevvo followed them, turning his head slowly. A Romero had appeared on the top floor. It stood in-between the two escalators looking across to the café. Bevvo slowly returned his view to his friend.

Geoff kept his hand in the stop position for a moment, not wanting to make any kind of movement the Dead might detect, then slowly lowered his fingers leaving the forefinger upright.

'*One.*'

He brought the finger to his lips.

'*Stay silent.*'

The Romero stood for a minute, possibly longer. Bevvo's stance was awkward and strained at his tendons, he had been caught mid-stride.

Geoff willed it to move. '*Fuck off.*' He finally dropped his finger from his lips. '*Go shopping you cunt.*'

The Romero, as though hearing Geoff's thoughts, stepped back from the railing. Hopefully it was going

to return to the dark department store and not decide to take a ride on the escalator like old times. It moved forwards again, turned, and headed for the Up escalator.
If it looked to the right they were screwed.
'*Oh shit.*' Geoff thought.
There was movement to his side, below. He peered over. A Romero had shuffled into view. It trudged on, not looking up, only ahead.
'*This is isn't good.*'
He slowly looked up to Bevvo again, who stood rigid, using his spear to balance him. His expression was one of expectation. Bevvo needed Geoff to figure this one out.
Geoff felt movement through his feet, then a line of sensation along his boot. A finger.
'*Seriously?*'
He twisted his torso to look behind and down at his ankle. A pale hand had pushed through the corpse pile and stroked at his heel.
'*At the side, below and behind. What's next, above?*'
He looked up. Above seemed Ok. Just the sun, that was however. dropping a little, the light barely pooling through the windows.
Bevvo slowly, deliberately tapped his wristwatch.
'*Hurry the fuck up!*'
Geoff nodded, his frustration evident.
The Romero on the stair halted. It swayed, its footing awkward on the bodies. It looked confused, as though it knew that something was not right with the escalator. Perhaps it didn't match the experience its primitive thoughts were sending it. It knew something was amiss.
Geoff thought of the annoyance he had felt back when the world worked, when he would head to the escalators in the Trafford Centre only to find them under maintenance. A real First World problem.

Perhaps this same memory had stopped the Dead on its journey.

It turned its head to face Bevvo. It saw him.

Geoff watched with widening eyes as Bevvo lifted his pole slowly and deliberately, he levelled it like a spear and pulled his arm back.

'*Christ, he's going to try and job it!*'

Geoff's jaw dropped. Bevvo was one for pranks, jokes and generally seeing how far he could push before someone pushed back, but this was quite possibly the dumbest thing he had seen Bevvo attempt. He raised his hand, palm flat, stiff with insistence.

'*STOP!*'

Bevvo didn't look at him. He didn't see Geoff's gesticulations or him mouthing the words, '*Don't be a twat!*'

The Romero lifted its arm, its fingers were messed up, possibly broken, perhaps they had once been wrought with arthritis. The thing looked like it might have been and old man, the forefinger was fixed in place as though pointing. As the things mouth stretched wide Bevvo was reminded of a movie he had seen, creepy as fuck, where aliens took over people when they were asleep, the guy in it, who was famous to him as someone's dad, but he had long since forgotten whose famous father he was, had turned out to be an alien at the end. He had pointed at this helpless woman and made an ungodly noise which would bring all of the aliens running to him.

Bevvo prepared to throw his spear at the Romero's head. He reckoned his chances of hitting it were probably one in a hundred, but it didn't look like Geoff was about to step up with a plan and he didn't have any other ideas.

The Dead stepped forward, tripped, lurched over and disappeared. There was a loud SMACK.

Bevvo looked to Geoff. Geoff raised his eyebrows. Bevvo inched forward to take a look towards where the Romero had fallen off the side of the escalator. It lay directly below where it had dropped. Its head was open, and a dark puddle formed around it.

'*Stupid is as stupid does.*' Bevvo thought.

He turned to Geoff and made the 'OK' sign with his thumb and forefinger.

Geoff exhaled and closed his eyes for a moment. He opened them up, making sure the last thirty seconds hadn't just been his mind playing tricks on him then looked over the side for the Romero that had wandered by, but it had continued its trek and was gone. He scanned the railings for any further guests and seeing none turned back to the task at hand, he stepped over the hand that grasped at his boot, its owner buried too deep to be a problem, and continued down the pathway of corpses.

Before reaching the final few feet Geoff slipped over the side wall of the escalator and quietly lowered himself down to the floor. Bevvo followed a few moments later.

They crouched, close up to the cover provided by the glass wall.

'Were you really going to throw that fucking thing?' Geoff said.

'Yeah, sure.' Bevvo shrugged, 'seemed like a good idea at the time. What was your plan? Engage it in some witty banter?'

'Cock.' Geoff said.

'You've lost your sense of sense of adventure mate. You are no longer dreaming the impossible dream.'

Geoff didn't reply. Instead he removed his backpack and opened it up.

As Geoff busied himself Bevvo glanced behind him, sensing someone watching. He saw a girl, he thought she must be about twelve or so, looking at him from the other side. Her eyes bulged a little and were bloodshot, her jaw worked at the padded elbow of a man who lay atop of her. His weight pushed the cloth of his jacket firmly into the girl's mouth. His elbows must have knocked her teeth down her throat and she was unable to chew at it effectively. Bevvo thought she must have been worrying at the thick material of the jacket for three years. She looked at him with hungry longing, but could only stare impotently. He looked away and began to dissemble his spear.

Geoff shuffled forward to take a brief look around the thick column concealing them.

'What's the story?' Bevvo asked when Geoff retreated from the column.

'Looks all right. Possibly even good. I counted six Romero's ahead. There's a couple of crawlers. No Dannys, not that I could see anyway.'

'Spread out?'

'Yeah, plenty of room to move. Can't say what it's going to be like further up, it curves to the right and if I remember rightly,' Geoff stopped talking and pulled out his map of the centre. He unfolded it and pointed to one of the orange blocks that represented each floor, 'right there. That's the front doors.'

'What d'you think Gee? Rope a Dope our way through?'

'No. It would take too long. We need to Butch and Sundance this.'

Bevvo drew in his breath as though he were about to give an estimate on a car repair. 'That's ballsy mate, you sure?'

Geoff nodded but only after a noticeable pause. 'There's safer options but they will all take time. The longer it takes us to clear our way to the front the more likely it is that others will wander in from outside. When they left the car park they were drawn by something. I'm ready to bet that the reason it's so clear down here is that a lot of the Deads from this floor were also tempted outside. But you know as well as I do they'll eventually wander back.'

'Any thoughts on that yet?' Bevvo asked

'What drew them? No.' Geoff said, putting his map away, 'but so far whatever caused them to move hasn't bit us in the arse and right now I'm treating it as a gift horse. But I can't shake the feeling that there's more than just Romeros out shopping today.'

'All right Gee, I'm game.' Bevvo said, as Geoff knew he would.

'We still have our out. There's nothing to stop us going back up these fuckers.' Geoff banged his head back lightly against the glass of the escalator. 'No Romero is getting up these. Even if we make a racket those on the far side of the next floor won't make it to us in time.'

'It would be a real shame to bail.'

'Yes, it would, so we're not going to. We've got this Bev. We just work through them to the doors, close em up and then it's just a sweep and clear mission all the way back.'

'Chew em up like Pacman.' Bevvo said, 'Wakka Wakka Wakka.'

Geoff raised his eyebrows.

'Sometimes, you are a very strange individual Mr Bevington.

'Says the man who calls a possibly suicidal option a Butch and Sundance.'

Geoff's lips twitched a smile.

'Gear up smartarse.'

'Roger that Captain Winter.'

92

Bevvo slid down from Geoff a little, giving them space to open their packs and prepare a smaller kit. The backpacks were far too big and cumbersome for what they needed to do. They would be left propped here at the bottom of the escalator, ready to be snatched up as they made their escape should it all go South.

Bevvo made sure to put his Morphine shots in his top jacket pocket. They had three of these each and they were worth a comparative fortune. If you had food, medicine was possibly the next most valuable commodity there was. His picks would remain holstered, it was time for the machete and knuckle dusters. The knuck's were another of Geoff's vicious engineering pieces. Four-inch nails were welded across the ridges. Just long enough to pierce the skull and damage the brain, but not so long that they got in the way.

He checked that each of his armour pads were secure. They were uncomfortable and encumbered him, but they confounded Deads who managed to get in close as they broke their teeth on the tough rubber. Finally, he took out his gun. A police issue, Heckler & Koch USP .45 calibre weapon prised from the hand of a Dead copper he had personally dispatched. The policeman must have been gripping the pistol when he was overwhelmed, and the magazine was empty. Bevvo had found an additional magazine affixed to the officer's belt.

Since acquiring it he had used two rounds of the twelve available in the magazine. Only two because gunshots were bad, very bad. Nothing bought the Dead out of the woodwork like the sound of gunfire.

'I'm good.' Geoff said.

Bevvo pulled the drawstring of his pack and fastened the covering flap down over it. 'I'm all set,' he replied, I'll start left, yeah?'

'Works for me.' Geoff said as he stood.

Bevvo noticed Geoff halt for a moment as he stood. It was clearly his knee. The solider had said nothing about it. It was probably some macho, military thing, but Bevvo hadn't missed the signs that his friend was having problems.

He wanted to talk to Geoff about it, but his friend left no opportune moment nor invited such a discussion. Geoff didn't do weakness. He didn't entertain failure or tolerate a negative attitude towards their survival. This was certainly not the time to question a man who he had witnessed killing another human being with his bare hands if he was feeling up to the task.

'Who are we?' Geoff asked, looking back to Bevvo.

'We're the Fucking Lemonade Brothers.' Bevvo replied, with determined calm.

'Damn right we are.' Geoff sniffed, breathed deeply and exhaled through his nose. 'Let's make some Lemonade.'

Bevvo nodded.

As one, they burst out from behind the column and into the wide shopping aisle, sprinting into the Deads ahead of them.

STICK TO THE PLAN

Manchester Airport
Three years earlier

Geoff veered away from the luggage cart and began to fire rounds into the oncoming Deads. The crowd turned as one, like flocks of birds that danced in the air, switching direction in unison. Seeing a human in the open, closer to them than the one half-hidden by the machine, was far more appealing. Geoff had learned that the Deads almost always went for the soft target.

'*Come on you pricks, ready meal, right here,*' He thought as he headed towards the terminal building, leading them away from the luggage car as Corky pushed its whining engine to its limit.

Corky saw that not all of the Deads changed their tack and went for the Captain. A single runner continued to charge at full tilt towards him, he raised his pistol ready to fire once his chance of shooting it in the face was at its optimum. To his surprise the things head exploded in a brief spray of glistening matter. It dropped.

Corky turned the car so he didn't run into the body, just in case some security measure installed for pedestrian safety stopped the thing. He looked to Captain Winter. It was his shot that had vaporised the running Dead's head. Winter had dropped to one knee and was firing three-round bursts into the creatures that ran.

The Captain had a name for them, in fact he had a name for each of the types of Dead they encountered. He called the slow fuckers Dannys and the fast ones were Romeo's, or something like that. The Captain certainly had some odd ways about him. However, since first joining up to the Army at aged seventeen he had fought alongside some of the finest soldiers in the world. Men and women whose bravery was awe inducing, but none of them held a torch to the Captain.

Winters obviously didn't want him, or any of the lads on the carts firing if they could help it. Corky had seen first-hand how gunfire brought the things in great number, almost as though they had been hiding and suddenly springing out at the sound of a firearm being discharged. He slipped his pistol back into his waist-band and focused on the path ahead.

Holstering the pistol, Geoff refreshed the clip of his assault rifle as he moved. Stopping was a risk. He only had seconds to present and fire and he needed to be accurate, there was no chance of him finding his target while on the move. Seeing the head of the Danny steaming towards Corky pop like a champagne bottle gave him a satisfying sense of relief. He quickly switched to the next nearest Dead to himself and calmly began to fire bursts, risking shots to the head while he still had some distance. He found his target on the first two and both instantly went sprawling into the tarmac. The rest had to be stopped via their legs.

Geoff sprayed each Dead until the rounds disabled them. No sooner had they hit the floor and discovered that standing was impossible, their shins or knees ruined or completely blown away, the Deads began to use their hands to pull themselves towards their prey. Geoff didn't question their commitment to their cause.

With the runners dead or downed there was only the horde of slow moving, shambling creatures to deal with. Most had moved away from the path of the luggage car and Corky was now free to proceed to the car park.

'I love it when a plan comes together.' Geoff said, in his best Hannibal Smith voice.

All he had to do now was let the Romeros get a little closer and he could run back to the luggage car as they dawdled behind him. He fired a few shots into the crowd as it came on, mostly to gauge the range, partially because it felt good. As he put a round expertly into the head of a tubby, shirtless Dead whose gut was open, its innards still slick and looking fresh something pulled at Geoff's thoughts about this.

'They don't rot. Even the horribly mauled appear to be fresh, as though having just being attacked.'

Lost in the implications, he barely caught the sound of breaking glass beyond the horde, but there was no missing the large plate windows on the upper floor of the terminal building as they exploded outwards and bodies fell with the fragmented sheets.

Geoff spun on his heels to face the scene. Deads were cascading to the floor, dozens upon dozens of them. The first few that dropped were smashed and disabled, but as the others dropped on top them the injuries they sustained didn't prevent them from rising. He saw that some twitched and spasmed as they rose.

'Oh fuck, more Dannys.'

He began to fire into them, aiming for the legs, hoping to keep the numbers down of those who could give chase, but still more fell from the windows. The cascade seemed endless, a waterfall of passengers, airport personnel and those drawn to the location through instinct. The assault rifle snapped onto an empty chamber and became silent.

Geoff stood, and ran.

Corky saw the windows explode. All along the terminal the sheer weight of the dead rushing to get to the source of the gunfire had caused them to press against the toughened glass. And despite its strength it had finally fractured and given in.

'Fuck me.' He said, and shouted behind him. 'Boys, are you seeing this?'

The canvas walls were slashed with sharp combat knives, and from each cart wide eyes stared out at the torrent of Deads falling from the building. Below it, Captain Winter knelt, firing into the bodies as they rose from the corpse pile forming at the base of the wall.

The horde of Deads continued to move towards the Captain, and in their shambolic, awkward version of a rush, they were spilling around unwittingly forming an enclosure around him.

The blade of a knife appeared through the canvas behind Corky's head and cut down. Thick fingers pushed through and pulled the flimsy wall apart. Rowley's face pressed up against the opened slit.

'We've got to help.' He stated.

This wasn't a request or a plea. Corky understood that if he didn't immediately put into action some kind of plan to assist the Captain, Rowley would do it by himself.

'Got any ideas?' Corky shouted, his mind raced, burning through options.

'Nope.' Rowley replied, and then disappeared from the hole in the canvass.

'Fuck.' Corky growled.

The Dead ignored him and his wagon train entirely now. The Captains gunfire had wrenched even the previously ignorant stragglers towards him. Turning the vehicle to the right still wasn't possible though, he would most likely just run into the swarm.

'Hang tight lads!' Corky bawled and spun the steering wheel to the left.

The little car turned, and the carts followed.

Corky's plan was basic, beat the Deads to the Captain, pick him up, leave. Which he thought was fine until the runners were factored in. Unless Geoff managed to pop every single one of them that fell from those upper floors they would be fucked, and that was bad. Definitely bad.

Straightening the car, and directing it towards the Captain, he hoped someone else within the team was ready to add to his staggeringly optimistic strategy.

He saw Captain Winter stand, pivot and begin to sprint away from the oncoming horde. To his relief Winter didn't head directly towards the car, instead he set off at an angle, away, allowing him to turn and present the length of the train of carriages.

Switching his attention to the Terminal for a moment Corky observed that the previous deluge of bodies falling from the windows had reduced to one or two late arrivals dropping down onto the broken mass below. Unfortunately, there were still runners amongst them. These fell, then stood, then ran at the lone figure pelting across the runway. With these new arrivals at least a dozen runners were active, and four of them gaining ground against the Captain.

They didn't tire these things. Corky had witnessed a runner chasing a couple on a motorbike once, from on high, within the bell tower of a village church in France. He watched the pair as they sped away across the vast, flat countryside surrounding the village. The single runner had not even begun to slow down until they had been long out of sight to it. Then it stopped and stood still. How long it had remained like that Corky couldn't say as he had been called to more pressing matters inside the village.

For certain, the distance between the luggage car and the Captain was too great. They were going to gain on him. Corky took his pistol from his belt once more. Turning the car again had brought the Deads much closer, and those further back had begun to break away from the crowd. Corky and his little train were now of interest once again.

'Come on you piece of shit.'

He cursed the luggage car. The accelerator pedal was flat to the floor, and had been like that for the whole time he had been driving it but it still only whined along at a steady ten miles per hour.

'Fucks sake Corky, faster.' Rowley's insistent voice came from behind him.

Corky didn't look back, he knew he would only see the fellow SAS man frowning at him.

'It won't go any faster ya cunt.' Corky snapped.

The was no retort from Rowley. He looked over his shoulder. Rowley was gone from the hole in the canvas.

Ahead Captain Winter had turned. Corky could see that he had shouldered his assault rifle, and figured that he must be out of ammo by now. The rifle was useless except as something to beat the Deads with. As he watched, Winters pulled out a pistol and fired rapidly.

'Come on… come on.' He said through gritted teeth, willing the cart to pick up speed.

The Captain had taken down two more runners, but three more were almost on him and the rest close behind.

Corky raised his pistol and was subsequently almost deafened, as the roar of automatic fire filled his ears. All along the luggage train the barrels of rifles had appeared and begun their percussive symphony of violence. Even with the restrictive vision of the canvas and awkward angle, the sheer volume of bullets meant that nothing within the wall of fire escaped impact.

The runners began to shred as they ran, blood and matter spewed from their bodies as rounds tore through them. In twos and threes they dropped to the floor. Some still crawled along afterwards but their immediate threat was gone.

Within only seconds the runners were ended. The fire then moved to the rows of slower moving targets close to the carts. The soldiers had played their hand, guns meant people, the luggage car was now fair game.

Geoff grunted with satisfaction as a round hit an oncoming runner squarely in the forehead. His shots to its legs had either missed, or impacted on its thighs, slowing it not at all. As it dropped it only revealed another directly behind it. They were gaining too fast, and there were too many.

He glanced towards the cart, it was approaching too slowly to get to him and with an army of Romero's trudging at its side. There was no rescue there, the Dead would have him before he could make it too Corky, and even if he somehow reached his colleagues all he would achieve is bringing the hordes attention to them.

He was done. He fired at the nearest runner, three rapid shots, all at the head, all missing entirely.

He thought of Angie, he thought of her long dark hair, he felt her strength and compassion and love.

He allowed himself to be taken to her in a memory, and the coolness of her finger as it traced a path across his cheek as they lay in bed, warm and safe. She tugged his beard and pulled his mouth to hers and they kissed deeply, arousing him, arousing her. When the kiss stopped she says, 'I love you' and he repeats her words. Geoff prepares to die with that thought in his mind. His love would handle the pain.

He had wanted to come back to England only to *see*, he had to *know*. Most accepted that their family, loved ones and friends were dead, but Geoff would not. No matter how irrational or pointlessly optimistic the idea that Angie might still be alive was he needed it to keep moving. If he found she was dead, that would be fine. He could stop then, he could end it and be at peace. But not until. At least not without trying. To have the opportunity snatched away by these things had always been a threat, and he accepted that without qualm. He was a soldier and suddenly being dead while in the pursuit of a goal was part and parcel of the job.

He would make it easy on the others though, he would keep running the Deads away, hopefully Corky would see that it was too late to save him and turn back towards the car park.

'*Fat chance.*' He thought, in the deepest, most rational corner of his mind.

British soldiers were notoriously stubborn and bloody minded. That's why they had so many dead heroes.

Geoff was startled as the runners coming to him vaporised in front of his eyes. Up until now, other than the sound of his own weapons issuing short blasts there had only been the smashing cacophony of the Terminal windows, and the low moaning hum of the Romero's. Now the air was filled with the report of automatic fire, and the sight of Deads being disassembled chunk by chunk.

His wits returned rapidly and he took advantage of the space created. Stopping to halt the runners had allowed the horde to move closer, and to spread, further blocking his path back to the car park. The luggage car was now moving directly towards him, parallel to the seething crowd, and the guns onboard had turned to the first few rows of Deads who, since rifle barrels had poked out of the canvas and unloaded into their colleagues, were very interested in the contents.

Geoff took a breath and began to run again. This time he didn't attempt to lead the Deads away, there was no point now, the cat was out of the bag.

Along the length of the train sprays of flesh erupted into the air as the lads expertly demolished the heads of the Deads clawing at the canvas as it passed them. Yes, the lads had definitely announced their presence.

Disaster came quickly, as it so often did when bravery stepped in for caution. Corky's little car was only six feet away when Geoff saw the back cart suddenly lift into the air a little. A Dead had fallen forwards and its upper torso slipped under the gap between its floor and the tarmac. As its small rubber wheels hit the body they stopped moving, the speed of the train, modest as it was, forced the final cart over the intruding body and with the timing that only the truly damned can expect, a surge of the Deads occurred, and they pressed their weight against the whole of the train. All of the carts withstood this but the last, the slight angle as it was pulled over the Dead produced instability. It wavered, then fully tipped.

Geoff increased his pace towards Corky, who was looking down at the simple control panel because a red light had appeared. Corly then looked up, questioning, only to see Geoff jump onto the front of the car and leap over his head to the roof of the first luggage cart.

Geoff hadn't been sure the canvas would take his weight, but it held firm despite having some give. He bounced across to the second cart without issue, but abruptly, the whole train came to a halt as he moved to the next in line. It threw his timing as he sprang causing him to miss-step. He fell flat, arms and hands splayed.

'*Oof.*'

The breath he had taken was expelled from his lungs. Below him, in car three, assault rifles were drilling into the horde. He lifted his face from the canvas and saw Deads climbing over the side of the final cart. As they scraped at the canvas wall, no doubt trying to tear the slash in it further apart, plumes of blood and spatters of gore danced about them.

Geoff stood, and continued his run across the train.

Corky Felt the shudder of the train just before it jerked to a halt. A red light illuminated on the dashboard, an exclamation mark printed on it suggested there was a problem but that was the limit of the information it offered.

'*What the fuck?*' he thought.

He looked up, Geoff was coming at him, but not going around, and suddenly the Captain leapt up onto the front of the car and over his head to the roof of the car behind.

'What... the fuck?' he gasped.

Checking himself, he examined the wires Geoff had snatched out, making sure they were still connected, and then punched the button. The red light stayed lit and the car remained stationary.

'Fuck me.'

He snatched up his assault rifle just as a Dead appeared at the side of the cart. It looked surprised but happy to see him. Corky blew its face off. He stepped back from the cart and as he exited saw the Deads begin to pour around.

'*Plan fucked. New plan required.*' He thought, and called out as he ran down the length of the train, slapping the sides of each of the canvas walls. 'Out lads, out! This side, this side.'

Ahead, he could see the last cart on its side. Anders had crawled out and was helping Shaw through the hole they had cut into the roof. Standing, with one foot on the edge of cart four's roof, and the other on the side panel of cart five was Captain Winter, pumping rounds into the Deads trying climb into the cart as the lads escaped.

Corky checked behind him and saw the others emerging through the side panels and then dropping to the floor. Deads were piling around the stationary train.

'Captain! Everyone's out.' He shouted up to Geoff, as he switched to a fresh pistol, having emptied his first.

'Alright, fuck it.' Geoff shouted back, 'Retreat, we'll have to lead them. We won't get through now.'

He jumped down from the cart, strode to Corky and drew up close, his face slick with sweat and red with anger.

'You should have stuck to the fucking plan.' He said, brushing past Corky, then began to fire at the Deads as they staggered towards them.

Corky took a breath, sucking in his desire to confront the Captain, 'Fuck you very much, you're welcome,' he muttered instead, as he approached Anders and Shaw.

'Come on you two, fucks sake. Those fuckers move slower than my Nan and she died ten years ago.'

He lifted his rifle and planted a bullet into the head of the first Dead to appear around the corner of the fallen cart.

Anders and Shaw jogged past him, heads down, and on to join with the others gathered around Captain Winter. As a group they began to back away, retreating to their starting point.

Geoff gave orders to only fire at runners. They could move quickly enough, even back-pedalling to avoid the Romeros. From his vantage point on top the carts he had seen more runners pelting through the terminal doors, and still more dropped from the windows. He could scarcely believe how many must have been inside the buildings. These new Dannys would be pushing their way through the horde.

'Keep em peeled lads,' Geoff said, 'anything breaks through or around that mob, fuck it up.'

A chorus of 'Roger that' issued from the group.

'I'm going to move on to point. Make sure we don't have a welcoming committee by the jets.' Geoff continued, and another series of acknowledgments sounded.

'I'm coming with.' Corky shouted.

Geoff nodded. 'Fair enough.'

They broke from the group and headed back towards the other side of the terminal building.

As they jogged Corky started, 'Sorry Captain. I just... didn't seem right to...' but was cut off sharply,

'Fuck it. It's done,' Geoff said firmly, 'Don't think I'm not grateful mate, but there's a bigger picture here.'

'Right Captain.' Corky replied, well aware that Winter was right. He could have gotten the lads to safety, the cost being one man for ten.

As they rounded the corner the sight of the haphazardly parked jets greeted them once again, but there was no sign on the Dead.

'Looks clear, I guess they were all drawn to the gunfire.' Geoff said.

'Think we can lead em around the terminal? Pick off the runners.' Corky asked, although he wasn't convinced. Just the short burst of adrenalin he had just experienced had caused him to feel a little dizzy. His hunger was starting to surface.

'Maybe.' The Captain appeared to be studying the aircraft.

'You don't think they'll manage the run.' Corky said, 'cramps.'

Geoff nodded slowly. 'Yeah, something like that.'

Corky understood what 'something like that' meant, they were close now, they had been through the mill, they were brothers. If one of them fell the others would go to their aid, just as he had instinctively done with the Captain. Their solidarity would kill them all.

The team came into view. Geoff and Corky turned to face them and shots rang out. Runners had burst through the trailing Romeros but were dealt with effectively.

Geoff looked back to the jets. 'I might have a new plan,'

'Oh yeah?' Corky looked about. 'Going to fly those fuckers all to Spain?'

'Nope. But hopefully somewhere hot.' Geoff replied. 'Run the lads down the taxi area. I'm guessing every Dead that's able is behind us now, it should be all right to go through the building. Double back on them.'

'They'll still be on our case though.' Corky said, not convinced.

'Maybe.' Geoff replied, not sharing his colleagues pessimism. 'How many grenades have you got?'

'Two.'

'I'll trade you.' Geoff said, and began to unbuckle his Bergen.

'Er... OK.' Corky replied, knowing better than to start questioning the Captain.

Geoff dropped the Bergen at Corky's feet and took the grenades. He placed them onto the floor along with his own, then opened the top of the pack and rooted around until withdrawing a roll of grey tape.

'Gaffer tape? You got a date?' Corky asked.

'I'm hoping for quite a bang,' Geoff replied. Neither man smiling at the exchange.

'Fuck me, you are one dangerous individual to be around.' Corky said, as Geoff knelt and began to tape the pile of grenades together.

'How long have we got,' Geoff asked, his focus on making his bomb.

Corky looked to the approaching horde. 'About thirty, forty seconds, can't see any runners.'

'OK, tell the lads to get a shift on. Full speed for about two hundred yards, then they need to get inside the terminal. I don't give a fuck how. Door, window, doesn't matter, make sure they get in and get low.'

'What the fuck are you going to do?' Corky asked with concern and suspicion.

Geoff looked up at Corky, his expression asking why he was still standing there.

'Aye Sir, on my way.' Corky said apologetically and ran towards the advancing team.

108

OOPS

Within seconds the lads came running past Geoff at the best speed they could manage with the heavy Bergen's, their tired muscles and the ache in their stomachs. They all looked at him, expressions of uncertainty painted across hard faces. He lightly nodded to each man. A salute.

Niemcyzk took the front, Corky the rear. He didn't look back to the Captain after passing him, instead he focused on the bigger picture.

Once they were past him Geoff took position further from the Terminal building, staying under the fuselage of the 747 looming above. His bomb was bulky, an awkward shape to throw, but it was also big enough to be a realistic target so long as he could see it. The Deads stumbled on, they were painfully slow but equally persistent. He eyed the long perfectly angled wing of the 747, pulled back his arm and hurled the cluster of grenades onto it.

His fear had been that it might roll or slide too far down the wing once it landed, but his lob had worked. The package hit the surface and remained still. It also didn't immediately explode, for which was extremely grateful.

He turned and jogged away from the horde, trying to maintain some distance from both them and the jet, but still keeping his bomb in sight. Once the Deads reached the fuselage of the 747 he wouldn't be able to risk making any more distance.

He was only about a hundred feet away when the nose of the next jet in line threatened to obscure his bomb. It was much closer than he had anticipated, but that was something he would just have to accept.

He lifted his assault rifle and took sight of the package.

There was only a mild breeze and he was close enough to have confidence in the shot. He allowed his eyes a single blink to clear them for the big moment.

The Deads reached the fuselage.

He fired.

The gaffer-taped package jumped a little, then landed a little further down the wing. Only a few inches, but enough to make the bomb a far smaller target.

'Fuck!' Geoff cursed.

He had hit the bundle but hadn't struck in a way that detonated the grenades. He drew his sight again.

The front of the horde moved on, past the nose of the 747, a moan rippled through it as the shot had echoed around the taxi area.

Geoff fired.

A miss.

His bullet passed uselessly by the bomb, a fraction of an inch to the right.

The Dead continued to move on, closing on him. He could stop now. Give it up, turn, run. He could easily outpace them.

Then, the first of the runners burst through the ranks. Then a second. Then a third. They came out of the horde like angry bees erupting from a hive.

Now he couldn't run.

He focused again.

Sighted what little of the bomb remained visible above the edge of the 747's wing.

He fired.

Geoff was accustomed to explosions. The detonation of charges, grenades, mortars and myriad other methods of small and large scale explosive destruction were no stranger to him, but he had never been this close to an incendiary blast, at least, not one he had created. He had no time to appreciate that his round had struck true, instead he only acknowledged the pain in his eye as the bloom of a fireball filled his vision. It was followed by a concussive blast lifting and throwing him backwards. His rifle left his hands as he was tossed through the air.

The roar of the explosion filled his ears and a series of loud bangs followed, as though the sun was cracking apart. The sound was accompanied by heat, further adding to the sensation. He hit the floor with a terrific thump to his back.

Geoff shook his head to clear the spinning, quickly regaining his senses, and got to his feet.

Just in time observe the army of Deads, now scattered and burning intensely, and to also see a flaming piece of ragged wing crash into its brother on the opposite side.

'Oops.' Geoff said.

He turned and ran.

He thought he might have heard the debris crash onto the other aircraft's wing, but with the general din of the leftmost wing continuing to puncture the air with blasts he couldn't be sure. No additional detonation occurred so far, but it was only a matter of time as fiery shards of 747 rained down around the other jets.

Geoff realised he hadn't quite thought past his objective of blowing the Deads to kingdom come and burning them to ashes with aviation fuel. But before he could begin to work out a contingency plan the delayed explosion finally arrived and boomed in his ears. This time the blast pushed at his back and he swung his arms wildly, trying to keep his balance. It almost worked. He still tumbled, but this time it was controlled, and he combat rolled out of the fall and was able to continue his sprint for safety.

Another terrific blast sounded and the airport erupted. The blasts were firing pieces of each jet into the plane next to it at ballistic speed. A domino effect was occurring. A British Airways 737 was lifted from the ground by the sheer force of the airbus exploding next to it.

Geoff saw none of this. Nor did he see the Deads vaporised as superheated fuel ate their skin, muscle and finally turned their bones to black sticks.

There was a double doorway ahead, it was closed, but every pane across the building had already been blown out by the concussive waves of the explosions. Geoff took advantage of this and turned, diving through a ragged hole framed by fragmented glass.

A boiling wall of flame pressed against the wall and shot through the door. Geoff rolled to the side, blindly hoping for cover to be available. Luck was with him. He crashed into an area where cases and bags had been abandoned, and although grunting as they toppled down onto his body he was shielded from the flames by them.

He stopped. Lay still, face pressed onto the floor, hands held under his chin. He waited for the chain of explosions and violent fireballs to run their course. He breathed in hot air, tainted with the bitter taste of aviation fuel and hoped he hadn't inadvertently blown his team to pieces. Then he heard the shouts, and the scream.

Geoff didn't look back at the wall of flame outside as the whole of the Terminal front burned. Instead, as soon as he had stood, he moved forwards, skipping over the cases and other baggage strewn about the place.

The light was poor inside, and once he had negotiated a few corners of the corridor he had to progress with a cautious pace. This was almost certainly a staff area, running underneath the lounge and embarkation areas above. Suddenly, red hot fingers of pain tore through his knee and upper thigh, he stopped and knelt, clamping his hands tightly over the incredibly painful area.

'Jesus!' He shouted, then cursed more quietly for making such a noise. 'Fuck me.'

He massaged the knee, trying to push the pain away and it did ease a little.

'Oh fuck.' Geoff gasped. *'Must have twisted it, must have banged it.'*

Visions of how and when the injury could have occurred zipped through his mind. For a solider he was old, at forty-nine he wasn't supposed to be doing this shit.

'Had to be the blast, had to be.'

He allowed himself exactly five more seconds of self-massage, then awkwardly continued on, limping badly.

The team were in the embarkation lounge; two flights of steps had bought them to a security door which fortune had left unlocked for them. It was gloomy here, despite light pouring in from the huge windows, now clear of their panes, where the Deads had poured onto the tarmac below.

Corky had guessed Winter was going to do something spectacular. The impromptu grenade-bomb had Die Hard written all over it, and the Captain's Field of Fucks to be Given was barren when it came to his own safety, at least compared to that of others. He hadn't been disappointed when he felt the whole terminal shudder from a series of massive explosions. Winters was clearly not a half-measures man.

Every window not already smashed or shattered crashed to the floor as each team member instinctively took cover. Flames boiled into the room sucking up the oxygen. Corky took three fast strides towards the counter of a burger restaurant, dived, and rolled around the curve of its frontage. For a few seconds Hell came to Earth in the embarkation lounge. He curled up as shards of glass, sticks of furniture and entire units flew past him. He remained still, forearms pressed against his face until he felt the wave of heat die down. Then someone screamed.

Corky gripped his rifle tightly, a finger hovering over the trigger, expecting to see a chorus line of Deads or an insane, hungry runner come flying at him. There was nothing, only dust falling from the ceiling and patches of flame licking at the floor, furnishings and walls.

He rose and scanned the room with his assault rifle presented. The others began to appear, popping up like extremely dangerous Meerkats. They looked about, looked to each other, trying to ascertain who screamed, who was missing.

The rounded twang of Niemczyk sounded.

'Here! here!'

Corky saw him advance, the Navy Seal had his weapon raised and sighted. At that moment Captain Winters burst through a door to the side of the burger restaurant.

'Corky.' Winters said, relieved to see his comrade. The Captain took in the scene in the lounge. 'Fucking hell. Did I do that?'

'Captain...' Corky said but stopped as the unmistakable sound of a suppressed shot from a heavy calibre weapon *thwunked* ahead.

114

'It's Niemczyk.' Corky advised. and pointed to where he had seen the Navy Seal go.

'Get to the others, round em up and get the fuck out of here.'

'Yes sir.' Corky replied.

Geoff pulled up his own rifle and ran towards Niemczyk, taking a brief look to the inferno beyond the broken observation windows.

As he pulled up to the Americans side it quickly became apparent what had caused him to call out. On the floor ahead was Anders, his neck a gaping hole with blood pouring from ragged edges. Anders stared up at the ceiling with surprised eyes. Close by him lay a Dead, the top of its head excavated by a shot from Niemczyk's silencer fitted rifle.

'Fuck.' Geoff said, he looked about for more Deads like this.

Its legs were chewed to the bone, almost every scrap of flesh was missing. A table had fallen, or perhaps been pushed onto them cracking the bones a little but not separating the legs from the things torso, and so it lay here, waiting with eternal patience, for someone to grab.

Geoff had seen this same thing in both Afghanistan and Paris, he had observed how trapped Deads adjusted to their circumstances. The ones that couldn't perform even their slow shuffle instead became quiet, and still, and struck like lightning as someone passed by. Geoff looked at its hands, they were almost black, the skin having hardened, allowing them to more easily rend their prey's flesh. The Dead had a grip of iron, but these, the trapped ones and the Crawlers who had similar disabilities but could still move about, required a crowbar or, as he momentarily recalled, a buzz saw to release their grip.

'Nothing I could do Captain. He was already gone. Must have been fast.' Niemczyk said, his delivery was professional, but Geoff could feel something like panic bubbling under his words.

Geoff pulled out his pistol.

'Take the lads around this. Corky's with them. We move as one, no one on point from here on.'

Niemcyzk glanced at the pistol, then turned and moved back to the team as they emerged from the cover they had sought.

Geoff reached behind his back and unclipped the silencer, then slowly screwed it into place. Anders didn't move. Sometimes the turn happened quickly, on occasion it could take days. With the muzzle in place and hearing the movement of the team above the steady roar of flames outside he fired a single shot into Anders head.

He was the first one he had lost since Paris, at least to the Deads. Others had succumbed to the effects of starvation but there was nothing he could do about that. He was determined not to lose any more, not today at least.

He looked to the right, Niemcyzk was leading the team on, accompanied by Corky. Geoff took a final look at Anders and moved to join them.

The car park would be just a road crossing from the end of the Terminal building. The Deads, with the exception of Crawlers, and those already trapped, had been drawn into his surprisingly effective ambush. It would bring more of them of course, that kind of noise guaranteed it, but that wouldn't matter as they would make for the source of it all.

The team would be all right. At least until malnutrition turned them into walking skeletons, and then who would know the difference between them and the Dead. And yes, he was going to leave them. Just like Ollie, their pilot, just like Omar had done in

Paris, he was going to leave the team, because he had to know whether Angie was dead or alive and every hour he spent headed in the wrong direction could be a fatal hour.

The team had their plan and that was good, whether he thought it had any merit or not. They were going to travel to the Manchester Medical Science Institute and see what good news the geeks had. If any were left alive.

'Always have a plan, stick to the plan.' It was his mantra.

He hoped they would make it. He hoped there was a cure. But they would have to make the trip without him. Corky was still able, Niemcyzk too, in fact Niemcyzk was very able, he thought. From the start something about the Navy Seal had set Geoff's nerves tingling, but he had let it slide because there were bigger problems than his own dark paranoia.

They reached the main entrance without further incident and crossed to the car park. There were Deads. Some slapped their hands against the bloodied windows of the cars they were trapped inside, a couple had been caught between vehicles mostly likely deliberately driven into them. But none were wandering. Geoff's fireworks had lured everything that could walk and crawl.

Rowley suggested heading to the Coach Park, which Geoff thought was a solid idea. There would be room for extra fuel and supplies and they quickly found a suitable vehicle, its driver lay in its doorway. His head had been smashed to a pulp, the keys were in the ignition.

'You should come.' Rowley said, as he stood opposite the Captain at the stairs to the coach. Corky was dragging the coach drivers body away and

117

Rowley kept his voice low. 'You haven't been sick. If there's still bods there they'll want to speak to you.'

'Yeah, I'm sure they will. Speak to me and lock me in a fucking Lab.'

'Not while we're breathing they won't.' Rowley stated with cast iron conviction. Geoff didn't doubt it.

'I'll come mate. I just have to get to Wilmslow. I've got to…'

'Yeah. I know.' Rowley cut in. 'Thought I'd give it a shot though.'

Geoff clamped a hand on Rowley's shoulder. 'I'll come.' He repeated, then dropped his hand and turned to leave.

'One thing though Captain. Just in case you don't.' Rowley said.

Geoff bristled. He knew what was coming. He turned to see Rowley's enquiring expression.

'Why were you in Afghanistan? The Yank isn't going to fess up. He still thinks there's a United States of America, but I'm fucking certain he was a part of whatever was going on there.'

Rowley, a mere five foot five, looked up at Geoff with eyes that he thought might be called puppy dog, if they weren't part of a man who could, and would kill you with his teeth if a mission required it.

'What the fuck was every special forces group on the planet doing in that fucking desert?'

Geoff had refused to be drawn on the matter while they had travelled and fought together, of why he, a senior and virtually retired officer had been assigned to the mess that was the Afghan conflict.

He took his office and oath seriously. But who was that oath to now? What was left to protect? There was only the team, they were all he could be sure existed of his former loyalties. Them and Angie.

118

'We weren't in Afghanistan. That was our cover.' Geoff said. Rowley's puppy eyes widened.

'Over the border?' Rowley asked

Geoff nodded. 'We were after books.'

'Books?' Rowley frowned.

Again Geoff nodded. He still couldn't find it in himself to just divulge the mission, at least not in one statement. Each admission was extracted from his mind with effort.

'Like... codes, plans... blueprints?' Rowley asked, seeing the resistance writ across his Captains face.

'No.' Geoff shook his head, something akin to a smile crept along his mouth. 'They were spell books.'

BUTCH AND SUNDANCE

Potteries Shopping Centre
Hanley

There were very few Deads and they were well spaced. Bevvo had drawn the short straw, having to sprint across to the far side of the row of stores without being seen, but he managed it without a hitch. Crouched at the corner of the recessed doorway to a Pandora Jewellers he looked across to Geoff, who nodded, held three fingers and began to fold them down into his fist one by one.

3...

Bevvo glanced ahead. A Dead shuffled on the spot about five feet away. It had barely moved, rather it swayed as it looked up at the USC clothing store signage that would have been illuminated with bright white lamps.

2...

Geoff's target was a woman, probably in her thirties. She had been savagely mauled and was bloodied from head to foot. Her intestines dragged at her feet, leaving a slug like trail of the slick black substance the things produced. She walked in a small circle and as such it suggested that this first push would be simple.

1...

It was. As one Bevvo and Geoff launched from their positions, making straight for their targets. Bevvo's ice pick smashed into his Dead's skull, the force he delivered after putting the full weight of his upper body into the swing took a chunk away. Glistening brain, stained bone and the black mucus spat at the air.

Geoff had opted for a machete and arced the blade across the eyes of the ruined woman. The bones were weak there, and his strength more than enough to almost cleave her head free from the bridge of her nose.

Both Deads dropped to the floor as one, but before the others, wandering mindlessly ahead could turn to investigate, The Lemonade Brothers had passed each other and switched hiding places.

They observed their handiwork for a moment. Ensuring that neither Dead had survived the assault. Satisfied, Geoff took out a wing mirror, a relic from an old Ford Escort, and angled it so he could see the situation ahead. The Deads hadn't noticed, or didn't appear to care that two of their number were now no longer window shopping. Geoff offered a thumbs up to Bevvo, who responded in kind.

The next attack would be a little more difficult. There were three in close proximity. All male, one of them had a skeletal arm that hung loose at its side but the others appeared to be fairly intact. Geoff looked to Bevvo and saw that the lad had two fingers up, he then pointed them at his chest.

Bevvo wanted to take out the two. Geoff considered refusing but checked himself. Bevvo had proven time and time again that he had the skills to handle exactly this kind of situation. It was tough, but he had to show the lad he had confidence in him. He angled the mirror again and observed the Deads wanderings. They appeared to be in no rush to move on, and further ahead the rest of them had their attention in shop windows or their feet.

Geoff held up five fingers this time. He wanted to make sure there were no surprise changes in attitude within the group. He began to fold his fingers.

5...

Bevvo pulled out his second ice-pick. He could see the reflection of his Deads in the large window across from him. They were close to each other, almost as though in conversation. Friends bumping into each other as they went about their shopping for a new jacket, or some jeans or maybe a gift for a loved one. Perhaps they were close because one had killed the other though, maybe it wasn't something so innocent, perhaps it was violence that had brought them together.

2...

Violence would end all of this for them and he would be the agent of it. He was good at this now, the destruction of them, and it was starting to concern him. Three years of obliterating these things, sometimes en-masse, but more often in this close up and almost personal way. It was becoming too easy, he wondered if he was beginning to enjoy it, and if so what did that say about him as a human being.

1...

Bevvo launched forwards, keeping low this time, out of the immediate eye-line of his Deads in case the one side-on caught sight of him. Geoff's route was easier. His Dead was shuffling forwards with its back to him. His blow would have to be brought down, and into the area where the skull was at its strongest, but he was a strong man.

They practiced these moves, set-pieces Bevvo called them as though they were a football team preparing for a weekend match. They studied their opponent's strengths and weaknesses, identified the star players and weakest line. This is why they were good, this was how they could enter the areas with the highest risks, but with the greatest rewards and come out with the goodies and their skins intact.

Bevvo pulled his arms back, as though he was playing jet fighters as he did as a child, he saw Geoff about to strike, his machete raised above his head, and the former solider looked terrifying, he was about to bring the blade down with enough power that the Dead's skull would pare apart like a melon.

As it happened, as Geoff's weapon came down, Bevvo lifted his ice-picks as one, and stood. The point of each entered the throats of the Deads and drove upwards and into the base of the skull, meeting the brain. It was a difficult attack to pull off and Bevvo felt pride in his ability to make it work, but the nagging question of whether he should feel this way floated into his thoughts again.

Their killing blows done they passed by each other once more and retreated to their new positions. Geoff quickly pulled out his mirror again and observed the scene ahead. A Dead had turned but didn't appear to have caught sight of them. It wobbled forwards a few steps, snapped its teeth together a couple of times, then began to walk back to the window it had been staring at previously.

He made the 'OK' sign to Bevvo, who replied with a nod. They could move up now, occupy the next set of opposing doorways and prepare to take out the final group, which milled around the front doors to the building.

Six more Deads lay between them and completing the first stage. Once the doors were shut and no more Deads could wander through, the centre was theirs. They could take out those remaining inside with impunity. They were close now. Very close.

To be continued...

Other writing by Eddie Skelson

Crowley: The Ravensblack Affair
Crowley: Mad Dogs and Englishmen
Crowley: By Day and By Night
Crowley: Crowley's Last Stand
The Collected Crowley

Winter Falls

Superhero City

The Whitby Horror and Other Tales

The Galvaston Chronicles: A Ballet of Bullets (out of print)
The Galveston Chronicles: Star Dallas (out of print)

The Lemonade Brothers: Dawn of the Dave
The Lemonade Brothers Books One and Two

Audio Books

Crowley: The Ravensblack Affair
Superhero City